May We Borrow
Your Husband?

ALSO BY GRAHAM GREENE

Novels

The Man Within
It's a Battlefield
The Shipwrecked (England Made Me)
Brighton Rock
The Power and the Glory
The Heart of the Matter
The End of the Affair
The Quiet American
A Burnt-Out Case
The Comedians

Short Stories

Twenty-one Stories
A Sense of Reality

Essays

The Lost Childhood

Entertainments

Orient Express (Stamboul Train)
The Third Man
Loser Takes All
Three by Graham Greene:
   This Gun for Hire (A Gun for Sale)
   The Confidential Agent
   The Ministry of Fear
Our Man in Havana

Travel

Journey without Maps
Another Mexico (The Lawless Roads)
In Search of a Character

Plays

The Living Room
The Potting Shed
The Complaisant Lover

Graham Greene

Cling to the virtues normally manifested by all Lebanese.

—Prime Minister Sami-as-Sulh

May We Borrow Your Husband?

AND OTHER COMEDIES

OF THE SEXUAL LIFE

NEW YORK / THE VIKING PRESS

Published in 1967 by The Viking Press, Inc.
625 Madison Avenue, New York, N.Y. 10022

Library of Congress catalog card number: 67–13500
Printed in U.S.A. by H. Wolff Book Mfg. Co.

Second printing May 1967

"Mortmain" first appeared in *Playboy* and "Two Gentle People" in *Vogue* as ("The Secret"). Other stories in this collection were first published in *Esquire, Rogue, Saturday Evening Post, Show,* and *Status.*

Contents

May We Borrow Your Husband?   3

Beauty   47

Chagrin in Three Parts   53

The Over-night Bag   63

Mortmain   73

Cheap in August   89

A Shocking Accident   123

The Invisible Japanese Gentlemen   133

Awful When You Think of It   139

Doctor Crombie   145

The Root of All Evil   155

Two Gentle People   173

May We Borrow
Your Husband?

May We Borrow
Your Husband?

I

I never heard her called anything else but Poopy, either by her husband or by the two men who became their friends. Perhaps I was a little in love with her (absurd though that may seem at my age), because I found that I resented the name. It was unsuited to someone so young and so open—too open; she belonged to the age of trust just as I belonged to the age of cynicism. "Good old Poopy"—I even heard her called that by the elder of the two interior-decorators (who had known her no longer than I had): a sobriquet which might have been good enough for some vague bedraggled woman of middle age who drank a bit too much but who was useful to drag around as a kind of blind—and those two certainly needed a blind. I once asked the girl her real name, but all she said was, "Everyone calls me Poopy," as though that finished it, and I was afraid of appearing too square if I pursued the question further—too middle-aged perhaps as well—so though I hate the

name whenever I write it down, Poopy she has to remain: I have no other.

I had been at Antibes working on a book of mine, a
biography of the seventeenth-century poet the Earl of
Rochester, for more than a month before Poopy and her
husband arrived. I had come there as soon as the full
season was over, to a small ugly hotel by the sea not far
from the ramparts, and I was able to watch the season
depart with the leaves in the Boulevard Général Leclerc. At first, even before the trees had begun to drop,
the foreign cars were on the move homeward. A few
weeks earlier, I had counted fourteen nationalities, including Morocco, Turkey, Sweden, and Luxembourg,
between the sea and the Place de Gaulle, to which I
walked every day for the English papers. Now all the
foreign number-plates had gone, except for the Belgian
and the German and an occasional English one, and, of
course, the ubiquitous number-plates of the State of
Monaco. The cold weather had come early and Antibes
catches only the morning sun—good enough for breakfast on the terrace, but it was safer to lunch indoors or
the shadow overtook the coffee. A cold and solitary Al-
gerian was always there, leaning over the ramparts, looking for something, perhaps safety.

It was the time of year I liked best, when Juan les Pins
becomes as squalid as a closed fun-fair with Lunar Park
boarded up and cards marked *"Fermeture Annuelle"* outside the Pam-Pam and Maxim's, and the Concours Inter-
national Amateur de Striptease at the Vieux Colombier
is over for another season. Then Antibes comes into its
own as a small country town with the Auberge de Pro-

4

vence full of local people, and old men sit indoors drinking beer or *pastis* at the *glacier* in the Place de Gaulle. The small garden, which forms a roundabout on the ramparts, looks a little sad with the short stout palms bowing their brown fronds; the sun in the morning shines without any glare, and the few white sails move gently on the unblinding sea.

You can always trust the English to stay on longer than others into the autumn. We have a blind faith in the southern sun and we are taken by surprise when the wind blows icily over the Mediterranean. Then a bickering war develops with the hotel-keeper over the heating on the third floor, and the tiles strike cold underfoot. For a man who has reached the age when all he wants is some good wine and some good cheese and a little work, it is the best season of all. I know how I resented the arrival of the interior-decorators just at the moment when I had hoped to be the only foreigner left, and I prayed that they were birds of passage. They arrived before lunch in a scarlet Sprite—a car much too young for them—and they wore elegant sports clothes more suited to spring at the Cap. The elder man was nearing fifty and the grey hair that waved over his ears was too uniform to be true: the younger had passed thirty and was as black as the other was grey. I knew their names were Stephen and Tony before they even reached the reception desk, for they had clear, penetrating, yet superficial voices, like their gaze, which had quickly lighted on me where I sat with a Ricard on the terrace and registered that I had nothing of interest for them, and passed on. They were not arrogant: it was simply that

5

they were much more concerned with each other, and yet perhaps, like a married couple of some years' standing, not very profoundly.

I soon knew a great deal about them. They had rooms side by side in my passage, though I doubt if both rooms were often occupied, for l used to hear voices from one room or the other most evenings when I went to bed. Do I seem too curious about other people's affairs? But in my own defence I have to say that the events of this sad little comedy were forced by all the participants on my attention. The balcony where I worked every morning on my life of Rochester overhung the terrace where the interior-decorators took their coffee, and even when they occupied a table out of sight those clear elocutionary voices mounted up to me. I didn't want to hear them; I wanted to work. Rochester's relations with the actress, Mrs. Barry, were my concern at the moment, but it is almost impossible in a foreign land not to listen to one's own tongue. French I could have accepted as a kind of background noise, but I could not fail to overhear English.

"My dear, guess who's written to me now?"

"Alec?"

"No, Mrs. Clarenty."

"What does the old hag want?"

"She objects to the mural in her bedroom."

"But Stephen, it's divine. Alec's never done anything better. The dead faun . . ."

"I think she wants something more nubile and less necrophilous."

"The old lecher."

They were certainly hardy, those two. Every morning around eleven they went bathing off the little rocky peninsula opposite the hotel—they had the autumnal Mediterranean, so far as the eye could see, entirely to themselves. As they walked briskly back in their elegant bikinis, or sometimes ran a little way for warmth, I had the impression that they took their baths less for pleasure than for exercise—to preserve the slim legs, the flat stomachs, the narrow hips for more recondite and Etruscan pastimes.

Idle they were not. They drove the Sprite to Cagnes, Vence, St. Paul, to any village where an antique store was to be rifled, and they brought back with them objects of olive wood, spurious old lanterns, painted religious figures which in the shop would have seemed to me ugly or banal, but which I suspect already fitted in their imaginations some scheme of decoration the reverse of commonplace. Not that their minds were altogether on their profession. They relaxed.

I encountered them one evening in a little sailors' bar in the old port of Nice. Curiosity this time had led me in pursuit, for I had seen the scarlet Sprite standing outside the bar. They were entertaining a boy of about eighteen who, from his clothes, I imagine worked as a hand on the boat to Corsica, which was at the moment in harbour. They both looked very sharply at me when I entered, as though they were thinking, "Have we misjudged him?" I drank a glass of beer and left, and the younger said "Good evening" as I passed the table.

After that we had to greet each other every day in the hotel. It was as though I had been admitted to an intimacy.

Time for a few days was hanging as heavily on my hands as on Lord Rochester's. He was staying at Mrs. Fourcard's baths in Leather Lane, receiving mercury treatment for the pox, and I was awaiting a whole section of my notes which I had inadvertently left in London. I couldn't release him till they came, and my sole distraction for a few days was those two. As they packed themselves into the Sprite of an afternoon or evening I liked to guess from their clothes the nature of their excursion. Always elegant, they were yet successful, by the mere exchange of one *tricot* for another, in indicating their mood: they were just as well dressed in the sailors' bar but a shade more simply; when dealing with a Lesbian antique dealer at St. Paul, there was a masculine dash about their handkerchiefs. Once they disappeared altogether for the inside of a week in what I took to be their oldest clothes, and when they returned the older man had a contusion on his right cheekbone. They told me they had been over to Corsica. Had they enjoyed it? I asked.

"Quite barbaric," the young man, Tony, said, but not, I thought, in praise.

He saw me looking at Stephen's cheek and he added quickly, "We had an accident in the mountains."

It was two days after that, just at sunset, that Poopy arrived with her husband. I was back at work on Rochester, sitting in an overcoat on my balcony, when a taxi drove up—I recognized the driver as someone who plied regularly from Nice airport. What I noticed first, because the passengers were still hidden, was the luggage, which was of bright blue and of an astonishing newness. Even the initials—rather absurdly PT—shone like newly minted coins. There were a large suitcase and a small suitcase and a hat-box, all of the same cerulean hue, and after that a respectable old leather case totally unsuited to air travel, the kind one inherits from a father, with half a label still left from Shepheard's Hotel or the Valley of the Kings. Then the passenger emerged and I saw Poopy for the first time. Down below, the interior-decorators were watching too, and drinking Dubonnet.

She was a very tall girl, perhaps five feet nine, very slim, very young, with hair the colour of conkers, and her costume was as new as her luggage. She said, *"Finalmente,"* looking at the undistinguished façade with an air of rapture—or perhaps it was only the shape of her eyes. When I saw the young man I felt certain they were just married; it wouldn't have surprised me if confetti had fallen out from the seams of their clothes. They were like a photograph in *The Tatler;* they had camera smiles for each other and an underlying nervousness. I was sure they had come straight from the reception, and that it had been a smart one, after a proper church wedding.

They made a very handsome couple as they hesitated a moment before going up the steps to the reception. The long beam of the Phare de la Garoupe brushed the water behind them, and the floodlighting went suddenly on outside the hotel as if the manager had been waiting for their arrival to turn it up. The two decorators sat

there without drinking, and I noticed that the elder one
had covered the contusion on his cheek with a very
clean white handkerchief. They were not, of course,
looking at the girl, but at the boy. He was over six feet
tall and as slim as the girl, with a face that might have
been cut on a coin, completely handsome and completely dead—but perhaps that was only an effect of his
nerves. His clothes, too, I thought, had been bought for
the occasion, the sports jacket with a double slit and
the grey trousers cut a little narrowly to show off the
long legs. It seemed to me that they were both too
young to marry—I doubt if they had accumulated forty-
five years between them—and I had a wild impulse to
lean over the balcony and warn them away—"Not this
hotel. Any hotel but this." Perhaps I could have told
them that the heating was insufficient or the hot water
erratic or the food terrible, not that the English care
much about food, but of course they would have paid
me no attention—they were so obviously "booked," and
what an ageing lunatic I should have appeared in their
eyes. ("One of those eccentric English types one finds
abroad"—I could imagine the letter home.) This was the
first time I wanted to interfere, and I didn't know them
at all. The second time it was already too late, but I
think that I shall always regret that I did not give way to
that madness. . . .

It had been the silence and attentiveness of those
two down below which had frightened me, and the
patch of white handkerchief hiding the shameful contusion. For the first time too I heard the hated name:
"Shall we see the room, Poopy, or have a drink first?"

They decided to see the room, and the two glasses of Dubonnet clicked again into action.

I think she had more idea of how a honeymoon should be conducted than he had, because they were not seen again that night.

II

I was late for breakfast on the terrace, but I noticed that Stephen and Tony were lingering longer than usual. Perhaps they had decided at last that it was too cold for a bathe; I had the impression, however, that they were lying in wait. They had never been so friendly to me before, and I wondered whether perhaps they regarded me as a kind of cover, with my distressingly normal appearance. My table for some reason that day had been shifted and was out of the sun, so Stephen suggested that I should join theirs; they would be off in a moment, after one more cup. . . . The contusion was much less noticeable today, but I think he had been applying powder.

"You staying here long?" I asked them, conscious of how clumsily I constructed a conversation compared with their easy prattle.

"We had meant to leave tomorrow," Stephen said, "but last night we changed our minds."

"Last night?"

"It was such a beautiful day, wasn't it? Oh, I said to Tony, surely we can leave poor dreary old London a little longer. It has an awful staying power—like a railway sandwich."

"Are your clients so patient?"

"My dear, the clients? You never in your life saw such atrocities as we get from Brompton Square and like venue. It's always the way. People who pay others to decorate for them have ghastly taste themselves."

"You do the world a service, then. Think what we might suffer without you. In Brompton Square."

Tony giggled. "I don't know how we'd stand it if we hadn't our private jokes. For example, in Mrs. Clarenty's case, we've installed what we call the Loo of Lucullus."

"She was enchanted," Stephen said.

"The most obscene vegetable form. It reminded me of a harvest festival."

They suddenly became very silent and attentive, watching somebody over my shoulder. I looked back. It was Poopy, all by herself. She stood there, waiting for the boy to show her which table she could take, like a new girl at school who doesn't know the rules. She even seemed to be wearing a school uniform: very tight trousers, slit at the ankle—but she hadn't realized that the summer term was over. She had dressed up like that, I felt certain, so as not to be noticed, in order to hide herself, but there were only two other women on the terrace and they were both wearing sensible tweed skirts. She looked at them nostalgically as the waiter led her past our table to one nearer the sea. Her long legs moved awkwardly in the pants as though they felt exposed.

"The young bride," Tony said.

"Deserted already," Stephen said with extreme satisfaction.

12

"Her name is Poopy Travis, you know."

"It's an extraordinary name to choose. She couldn't have been *christened* that way, unless they found a very liberal vicar."

"He is called Peter. Of an undefined occupation. Not army, I think, do you?"

"Oh, no, not army. Something to do with land perhaps —there's an agreeable *herbal* smell about him."

"You seem to know nearly all there is to know," I said.

"We looked at their police *carnet* before dinner."

"I have an idea," Tony said, "that PT hardly represents their activities last night." He looked across the tables at the girl with an expression extraordinarily like hatred.

"We were both taken," Stephen said, "by the air of innocence. One felt he was more used to horses."

"He mistook the yearnings of the rider's crotch for something quite different."

Perhaps they hoped to shock me, but I don't think it was that. I really believe they were in a state of extreme sexual excitement; they had received a *coup de foudre* last night on the terrace and were quite incapable of disguising their feelings. I was an excuse to talk, to speculate about the desired object. The sailor had been a stopgap; this was the real thing. I was inclined to be amused, for what could this absurd pair hope to gain from a young man newly married to the girl who now sat there patiently waiting, wearing her beauty like an old sweater she had forgotten to change? But that was a bad simile to use: she would have been afraid to wear an old sweater, except secretly, by herself, in the playroom. She had no idea that she was one of those who can afford to disregard the fashion of their clothes. She caught my eye and, because I was so obviously English, I suppose, gave me half a timid smile. Perhaps I too would have received the *coup de foudre* if I had not been thirty years older and twice married.

Tony detected the smile. "A regular body-snatcher," he said. My breakfast and the young man arrived at the same moment before I had time to reply. As he passed the table I could feel the tension.

"*Cuir de Russie*," Stephen said, quivering a nostril. "A mistake of inexperience."

The youth caught the words as he went past and turned with an astonished look to see who had spoken, and they both smiled insolently back at him as though they really believed they had the power to take him over. . . .

For the first time I felt disquiet.

III

Something was not going well; that was sadly obvious. The girl nearly always came down to breakfast ahead of her husband—I have an idea he spent a long time bathing and shaving and applying his *Cuir de Russie*. When he joined her he would give her a courteous brotherly kiss as though they had not spent the night together in the same bed. She began to have those shadows under the eyes which come from lack of sleep—for I couldn't believe that they were "the lineaments of gratified desire." Sometimes from my balcony I saw them returning from a walk—nothing, except perhaps a pair of horses, could have been more handsome. His gentleness towards her might have reassured her mother, but it made a man impatient to see him squiring her across the undangerous road, holding open doors, following a pace behind her like the husband of a princess. I longed to see some outbreak of irritation caused by the sense of satiety, but they never seemed to be in conversation when they returned from their walk, and at table I caught only the kind of phrases people use who are dining together for the sake of politeness. And yet I could swear that she loved him, even by the way she avoided watching him. There was nothing avid or starved about her; she stole her quick glances when she was quite certain that his attention was absorbed elsewhere—they were tender, anxious perhaps, quite undemanding. If one inquired after him when he wasn't there, she glowed with the pleasure of using his name. "Oh, Peter overslept this morning." "Peter cut himself. He's staunching the blood now." "Peter's mislaid his tie. He thinks the floor-waiter has purloined it." Certainly she loved him; I was far less certain of what his feelings were.

And you must imagine how all the time those other two were closing in. It was like a mediaeval siege: they dug their trenches and threw up their earthworks. The difference was that the besieged didn't notice what they were at—at any rate, the girl didn't; I don't know about him. I longed to warn her, but what could I have said that wouldn't have shocked her or angered her? I believe the two would have changed their floor if that would have helped to bring them closer to the fortress; they probably discussed the move together and decided against it as too overt.

Because they knew that I could do nothing against them, they regarded me almost in the role of an ally. After all, I might be useful one day in distracting the girl's attention—and I suppose they were not quite mistaken in that; they could tell from the way I looked at her how interested I was, and they probably calculated that my interests might in the long run coincide with theirs. It didn't occur to them that, perhaps, I was a man with scruples. If one really wanted a thing scruples were obviously, in their eyes, out of place. There was a tortoiseshell star mirror at St. Paul they were plotting to obtain for half the price demanded (I think there was an old mother who looked after the shop when her daughter was away at a *boîte* for women of a certain taste); naturally, therefore, when I looked at the girl, as they saw me so often do, they considered I would be ready to join in any "reasonable" scheme.

"When I looked at the girl"—I realize that I have made no real attempt to describe her. In writing a biography one can, of course, just insert a portrait and the affair is done: I have the prints of Lady Rochester and Mrs. Barry in front of me now. But speaking as a professional novelist (for biography and reminiscence are both new forms to me), one describes a woman not so much that the reader should see her in all the cramping detail of colour and shape (how often Dickens's elaborate portraits seem like directions to the illustrator which might well have been left out of the finished book), but to convey an emotion. Let the reader make his own image of a wife, a mistress, some passerby "sweet and kind" (the poet required no other descriptive words), if he has a fancy to. If I were to describe the girl (I can't bring myself at this moment to write her hateful name), it would not be to convey the colour of her hair, the shape of her mouth, but to express the pleasure and the pain with which I recall her—I, the writer, the observer, the subsidiary character, what you will. But if I didn't bother to convey them to her, why should I bother to convey them to you, *hypocrite lecteur?*

How quickly those two tunneled. I don't think it was more than four mornings after the arrival that, when I came down to breakfast, I found they had moved their table next to the girl's and were entertaining her in her husband's absence. They did it very well; it was the first time I had seen her relaxed and happy—and she was happy because she was talking about Peter. Peter was agent for his father, somewhere in Hampshire—there were three thousand acres to manage. Yes, he was fond of riding and so was she. It all tumbled out—the kind of life she dreamed of having when she returned home. Stephen just dropped in a word now and then, of a rather old-fashioned courteous interest, to keep her going. Apparently he had once decorated some Hall in their neighborhood and knew the names of some people Peter knew—Winstanley, I think—and that give her immense confidence.

"He's one of Peter's best friends," she said, and the two flickered their eyes at each other like lizards' tongues.

"Come and join us, William," Stephen said, but only when he had noticed that I was within earshot. "You know Mrs. Travis?"

How could I refuse to sit at their table? And yet in doing so I seemed to become an ally.

"Not *the* William Harris?" the girl asked. It was a phrase which I hated, and yet she transformed even that, with her air of innocence. For she had a capacity to make everything new: Antibes became a discovery and we were the first foreigners to have made it. When she said, "Of course, I'm afraid I haven't actually *read* any of your books," I heard the over-familiar remark for the first time; it even seemed to me a proof of her honesty—I nearly wrote her virginal honesty. "You must know an awful lot about people," she said, and again I read into the banality of the remark an appeal— for help against whom, those two or the husband, who at that moment appeared on the terrace? He had the same nervous air as she, even the same shadows under the lids, so that they might have been taken by a stranger, as I wrote before, for brother and sister. He hesitated a moment when he saw all of us there and she called across to him, "Come and meet these nice people, darling." He didn't look any too pleased, but he sat glumly down and asked whether the coffee was still hot.

"I'll order some more, darling. They know the Winstanleys, and this is *the* William Harris."

He looked at me blankly; I think he was wondering if I had anything to do with tweeds.

"I hear you like horses," Stephen said, "and I was wondering whether you and your wife would come to lunch with us at Cagnes on Saturday. That's tomorrow, isn't it? There's a very good racecourse at Cagnes. . . ."

"I don't know," he said dubiously, looking to his wife for a clue.

"But, darling, of course we must go. You'd love it."

His face cleared instantly. I really believe he had been troubled by a social scruple: the question whether one accepts invitations on a honeymoon. "It's very good of you," he said, "Mr.—"

"Let's start as we mean to go on. I'm Stephen and this is Tony."

"I'm Peter." He added a trifle gloomily, "And this is Poopy."

"Tony, you take Poopy in the Sprite, and Peter and I will go by *autobus*." (I had the impression, and I think Tony had too, that Stephen had gained a point.)

"You'll come too, Mr. Harris?" the girl asked, using my surname as though she wished to emphasize the difference between me and them.

"I'm afraid I can't. I'm working against time."

I watched them that evening from my balcony as they returned from Cagnes and hearing the way they all laughed together I thought, The enemy are within the citadel: it's only a question of time. A lot of time, because they proceeded very carefully, those two. There was no question of a quick grab, which I suspect had caused the contusion in Corsica.

IV

It became a regular habit with the two of them to enter-
tain the girl during her solitary breakfast before her
husband arrived. I never sat at their table again, but
scraps of the conversation would come over to me, and it
seemed to me that she was never quite so cheerful again.
Even the sense of novelty had gone. I heard her say
once, "There's so little to do here," and it struck me as an
odd observation for a honeymooner to make.

Then one evening I found her in tears outside the
Musée Grimaldi. I had been fetching my papers, and as
my habit was, I made a round by the Place Nationale
with the pillar erected in 1819 to celebrate—a remark-
able paradox—the loyalty of Antibes to the monarchy
and her resistance to *"Les Troupes Etrangères"* who
were seeking to re-establish the monarchy. Then, ac-
cording to rule, I went on by the market and the old
port and Lou-Lou's restaurant up the ramp towards the
cathedral and the Musée, and there in the grey evening
light, before the street-lamps came on, I found her
crying under the cliff of the château.

I noticed too late what she was at or I wouldn't have
said, "Good evening, Mrs. Travis." She jumped a little
as she turned and dropped her handkerchief, and when
I picked it up I found it soaked with tears—it was like
holding a small drowned animal in my hand. I said, "I'm
sorry," meaning that I was sorry to have startled her, but
she took it in quite another sense. She said, "Oh, I'm

just being silly, that's all. It's just a mood. Everybody has moods, don't they?"

"Where's Peter?"

"He's in the museum with Stephen and Tony looking at the Picassos. I don't understand them a bit."

"That's nothing to be ashamed of. Lots of people don't."

"But Peter doesn't understand them either. I know he doesn't. He's just pretending to be interested."

"Oh, well . . ."

"And it's not that, either. I pretended for a time too, to please Stephen. But he's pretending just to get away from me."

"You are imagining things."

Punctually at five o'clock the *phare* lit up, but it was still too light to see the beam.

I said, "The museum will be closing now."

"Walk back with me to the hotel."

"Wouldn't you like to wait for Peter?"

"I don't smell, do I?" she asked miserably.

"Well, there's a trace of Arpège. I've always liked Arpège."

"How terribly experienced you sound."

"Not really. It's just that my first wife used to buy Arpège."

We began walking back, and the mistral bit our ears and gave her an excuse when the time came for the reddened eyes.

"She said, "I think Antibes so sad and grey."

"I thought you enjoyed it here."

"Oh, for a day or two."

"Why not go home?"

"It would look odd, wouldn't it, returning early from a honeymoon?"

"Or go on to Rome—or somewhere. You can get a plane to most places from Nice."

"It wouldn't make any difference," she said. "It's not the place that's wrong, it's me."

"I don't understand."

"He's not happy with me. It's as simple as that."

She stopped opposite one of the little rock houses by the ramparts. Washing hung down over the street below and there was a cold-looking canary in a cage.

"You said yourself . . . a mood . . ."

"It's not his fault," she said. "It's me. I expect it seems very stupid to you, but I never slept with anyone before I married." She gulped miserably at the canary.

"And Peter?"

"He's terribly sensitive," she said, and added quickly, "That's a good quality. I wouldn't have fallen in love with him if he hadn't been."

"If I were you, I'd take him home—as quickly as possible." I couldn't help the words sounding sinister, but she hardly heard them. She was listening to the voices that came nearer down the ramparts—to Stephen's gay laugh. "They're very sweet," she said. "I'm glad he's found friends."

How could I say that they were seducing Peter before her eyes? And in any case, wasn't her mistake already irretrievable? Those were two of the questions

which haunted the hours, dreary for a solitary man, of
the middle afternoon when work is finished and the
exhilaration of the wine at lunch, and the time for the
first drink has not yet come and the winter heating is at
its feeblest. Had she no idea of the nature of the young
man she had married? Had he taken her on as a blind or
as a last desperate throw for normality? I couldn't bring
myself to believe that. There was a sort of innocence
about the boy which seemed to justify her love, and I
preferred to think that he was not yet fully formed, that
he had married honestly and it was only now that he
found himself on the brink of a different experience. And
yet if that were the case the comedy was all the crueller.
Would everything have gone normally well if some con-
junction of the planets had not crossed their honeymoon
with that hungry pair of hunters?

I longed to speak out, and in the end I did speak, but
not, so it happened, to her. I was going to my room and
the door of one of theirs was open, and I heard again
Stephen's laugh—a kind of laugh which is sometimes
with unintentional irony called infectious; it maddened
me. I knocked and went in. Tony was stretched on a
double bed and Stephen was "doing" his hair, holding a
brush in each hand and meticulously arranging the grey
waves on either side. The dressing table had as many
pots on it as a woman's.

"You really mean he told you that?" Tony was saying.
"Why, how are you, William? Come in. Our young
friend has been confiding in Stephen. Such really fasci-
nating things."

"Which of your young friends?" I asked.

"Why, Peter, of course. Who else? The secrets of married life."

"I thought it might have been your sailor."

"Naughty!" Tony said. "But *touché* too, of course."

"I wish you'd leave Peter alone."

"I don't think he'd like that," Stephen said. "You can see that he hasn't quite the right tastes for this sort of honeymoon."

"Now, you happen to like women, William," Tony said. "Why not go after the girl? It's a grand opportunity. She's not getting what I believe is vulgarly called her greens." Of the two he was easily the more brutal. I wanted to hit him, but this is not the century for that kind of romantic gesture, and anyway he was stretched out flat upon the bed. I said feebly enough—I ought to have known better than to have entered into a debate with those two—"She happens to be in love with him."

"I think Tony is right and she would find more satisfaction with you, William dear," Stephen said, giving a last flick to the hair over his right ear—the contusion was quite gone now. "From what Peter has said to me, I think you'd be doing a favour to both of them."

"Tell him what Peter said, Stephen."

"He said that from the very first there was a kind of hungry femininity about her which he found frightening and repulsive. Poor boy—he was really trapped into this business of marriage. His father wanted heirs—he breeds horses too—and then her mother—there's quite a lot of lucre with that lot. I don't think he had any idea of—of the Shape of Things to Come." Stephen shuddered into the glass and then regarded himself with satisfaction.

Even today I have to believe for my own peace of mind that the young man had not really said those monstrous things. I believe, and hope, that the words were put into his mouth by that cunning dramatizer, but there is little comfort in the thought, for Stephen's inventions were always true to character. He even saw through my apparent indifference to the girl and realized that Tony and he had gone too far; it wouldn't suit their purpose if I were driven to the wrong kind of action, or if, by their crudities, I lost my interest in Poopy.

"Of course," Stephen said, "I'm exaggerating. Undoubtedly he felt a bit amorous before it came to the point. His father would describe her, I suppose, as a fine filly."

"What do you plan to do with him?" I asked. "Do you toss up, or does one of you take the head and the other the tail?"

Tony laughed. "Good old William. What a clinical mind you have."

"And suppose," I said, "I went to her and recounted this nice conversation?"

"My dear, she wouldn't even understand. She's incredibly innocent."

"Isn't he?"

"I doubt it—knowing our friend Colin Winstanley. But it's still a moot point. He hasn't given himself away yet."

"We are planning to put it to the test one day soon," Stephen said.

25

"A drive in the country," Tony said. "The strain's telling on him, you can see that. He's even afraid to take a siesta for fear of unwanted attentions."

"Haven't you *any* mercy?" It was an absurd, old-fashioned word to use to those two sophisticates. I felt more than ever square. "Doesn't it occur to you that you may ruin her life—for the sake of your little game?"

"We can depend on you, William," Tony said, "to give her creature comforts."

Stephen said, "It's no game. You should realize we are serving *him*. Think of the life that he would lead—with all those soft contours lapping him around." He added, "Women always remind me of a damp salad—you know, those faded bits of greenery positively swimming. . . ."

"Every man to his taste," Tony said. "But Peter's not cut out for that sort of life. He's very sensitive," he said, using the girl's own words. There wasn't any more I could think of to say.

V

You will notice that I play a very unheroic part in this comedy. I could have gone direct, I suppose, to the girl and given her a little lecture on the facts of life, beginning gently with the régime of an English public school —he had worn a scarf of old-boy colours, until Tony had said to him one day at breakfast that he thought the puce stripe was an error of judgment. Or perhaps I could have protested to the boy himself, but if Stephen had spoken the truth and he was under a severe nervous strain, my intervention would hardly have helped to ease it. There was no move I could make. I had just to sit there and watch while they made the moves carefully and adroitly towards the climax.

It came three days later at breakfast when, as usual, she was sitting alone with them, while her husband was upstairs with his lotions. They had never been more charming or more entertaining. As I arrived at my table they were giving her a really funny description of a house in Kensington that they had decorated for a dowager duchess who was passionately interested in the Napoleonic wars. There was an ashtray, I remember, made out of a horse's hoof, guaranteed—so the dealer said—by Apsley House to have belonged to a grey ridden by Wellington at the Battle of Waterloo; there was an umbrella stand made out of a shell-case found on the field of Austerlitz; a fire-escape made of a scaling ladder from Badajoz. She had lost half that sense of strain listening to them. She had forgotten her rolls and coffee; Stephen had her complete attention. I wanted to say to her, "You little owl." I wouldn't have been insulting her —she *had* got rather large eyes.

And then Stephen produced the master plan. I could tell it was coming by the way his hands stiffened on his coffee cup, by the way Tony lowered his eyes and appeared to be praying over his *croissant*. "We were wondering, Poopy—may we borrow your husband?" I have never heard words spoken with more elaborate casualness.

She laughed. She hadn't noticed a thing. "Borrow my husband?"

"There's a little village in the mountains behind Monte Carlo—Peille it's called—and I've heard rumours of a devastatingly lovely old bureau there—not for sale, of course, but Tony and I, we have our winning ways."

"I've noticed that," she said, "myself."

Stephen for an instant was disconcerted, but she meant nothing by it, except perhaps a compliment.

"We were thinking of having lunch at Peille and passing the whole day on the road so as to take a look at the scenery. The only trouble is there's no room in the Sprite for more than three, but Peter was saying the other day that you wanted sometime to have a hair-do, so we thought . . ."

I had the impression that he was talking far too much to be convincing, but there wasn't any need for him to worry: she saw nothing at all. "I think it's a marvellous idea," she said. "You know, he needs a little holiday from me. He's had hardly a moment to himself since I came up the aisle." She was magnificently sensible, and perhaps even relieved. Poor girl. She needed a little holiday, too.

"It's going to be excruciatingly uncomfortable. He'll have to sit on Tony's knee."

"I don't suppose he'll mind that."

"And, of course, we can't guarantee the quality of food en route."

For the first time I saw Stephen as a stupid man. Was there a shade of hope in that?

In the long run, of the two, notwithstanding his brutality, Tony had the better brain. Before Stephen had time to speak once more, Tony raised his eyes from the *croissant* and said decisively, "That's fine. All's settled, and we'll deliver him back in one piece by dinner-time."

He looked challengingly across at me. "Of course, we hate to leave you alone for lunch, but I am sure William will look after you."

"William?" she asked, and I hated the way she looked at me as if I didn't exist. "Oh, you mean Mr. Harris?"

I invited her to have lunch with me at Lou-Lou's in the old port—I couldn't very well do anything else—and at that moment the laggard Peter came out onto the terrace. She said quickly, "I don't want to interrupt your work. . . ."

"I don't believe in starvation," I said. "It has to be interrupted for meals."

Peter had cut himself again shaving and had a large blob of cottonwool stuck on his chin: it reminded me of Stephen's contusion. I had the impression, while he stood there waiting for someone to say something to him, that he knew all about the conversation; it had been carefully rehearsed by all three, the parts allotted, the unconcerned manner practised well beforehand, even the bit about the food. . . . Now somebody had missed a cue, so I spoke.

"I've asked your wife to lunch at Lou-Lou's," I said. "I hope you don't mind."

I would have been amused by the expression of quick relief on all three faces if I had found it possible to be amused by anything at all in the situation.

VI

"And you didn't marry again after she left?"

"By that time I was getting too old to marry."

"Picasso does it."

"Oh, I'm not quite as old as Picasso."

The silly conversation went on against a background of fishing-nets draped over a wallpaper with a design of wine bottles—interior-decoration again. Sometimes I longed for a room which had simply grown that way like the lines on a human face. The fish soup steamed away between us, smelling of garlic. We were the only guests there. Perhaps it was the solitude, perhaps it was the directness of her question, perhaps it was only the effect of the *rosé*, but quite suddenly I had the comforting sense that we were intimate friends. "There's always work," I said, "and wine and a good cheese."

"I couldn't be that philosophical if I lost Peter."

"That's not likely to happen, is it?"

"I think I'd die," she said, "like someone in Christina Rossetti."

"I thought nobody of your generation read her."

If I had been twenty years older, perhaps, I could have explained that nothing is quite as bad as that, that at the end of what is called "the sexual life," the only love which has lasted is the love that has accepted everything, every disappointment, every failure and every betrayal, which has accepted even the sad fact that in the end there is no desire so deep as the simple desire for companionship.

She wouldn't have believed me. She said, "I used to weep like anything at that poem about 'Passing Away.' Do you write sad things?"

"The biography I am writing now is sad enough. Two people tied together by love and yet one of them incapable of fidelity. The man dead of old age, burnt-out, at less than forty, and a fashionable preacher lurking by the bedside to snatch his soul. No privacy even for a dying man: the bishop wrote a book about it."

An Englishman who kept a chandler's shop in the old port was talking at the bar, and two old women who were part of the family knitted at the end of the room. A dog trotted in and looked at us and went away again with its tail curled.

"How long ago did all that happen?"

"Nearly three hundred years."

"It sounded quite contemporary. Only now it would be the man from the *Mirror* and not a bishop."

"That's why I wanted to write it. I'm not really interested in the past. I don't like costume pieces."

Winning someone's confidence is rather like the way some men set about seducing a woman; they circle a long way from their true purpose, they try to interest and amuse until finally the moment comes to strike. It came, so I wrongly thought, when I was adding up the bill. She said, "I wonder where Peter is at this moment," and I was quick to reply, "What's going wrong between the two of you?"

She said, "Let's go."

"I've got to wait for my change."

It was always easier to get served at Lou-Lou's than to

pay the bill. At that moment everyone always had a habit of disappearing: the old woman (her knitting abandoned on the table), the aunt who helped to serve, Lou-Lou herself, her husband in his blue sweater. If the dog hadn't gone already he would have left at that moment.

I said, "You forget—you told me that he wasn't happy."

"Please, please find someone and let's go."

So I disinterred Lou-Lou's aunt from the kitchen and paid. When we left, everyone seemed to be back again, even the dog.

Outside I asked her whether she wanted to return to the hotel.

"Not just yet—but I'm keeping you from your work."

"I never work after drinking. That's why I like to start early. It brings the first drink nearer."

She said she had seen nothing of Antibes but the ramparts and the beach and the lighthouse, so I walked her around the small narrow back streets where the washing hung out of the windows as in Naples and there were glimpses of small rooms overflowing with children and grandchildren; stone scrolls were carved over the ancient doorways of what had once been noblemen's houses; the pavements were blocked by barrels of wine and the streets by children playing at ball. In a low room on a ground floor a man sat painting the horrible ceramics which would later go to Vallauris to be sold to tourists in Picasso's old stamping-ground—spotted pink frogs and mauve fish and pigs with slits for coins.

She said, "Let's go back to the sea." So we returned

to a patch of hot sun on the bastion, and again I was tempted to tell her what I feared, but the thought that she might watch me with the blankness of ignorance deterred me. She sat on the wall and her long legs in the tight black trousers dangled down like Christmas stockings. She said, "I'm not sorry that I married Peter," and I was reminded of a song Edith Piaf sings, "*Je ne regrette rien.*" It is typical of such a phrase that it is always sung or spoken with defiance.

I could only say again, "You ought to take him home," but I wondered what would have happened if I had said, "You are married to a man who only likes men and he's off now picnicking with his boy-friends. I'm thirty years older than you, but at least I have always preferred women and I've fallen in love with you and we could still have a few good years together before the time comes when you want to leave me for a younger man." All I said was, "He probably misses the country— and the riding."

"I wish you were right, but it's really worse than that."

Had she, after all, realized the nature of her problem? I waited for her to explain her meaning. It was a little like a novel which hesitates on the verge between comedy and tragedy. If she recognized the situation it would be a tragedy; if she were ignorant it was a comedy, even a farce—a situation between an immature girl too innocent to understand and a man too old to have the courage to explain. I suppose I have a taste for tragedy. I hoped for that.

She said, "We didn't really know each other much

before we came here. You know, weekend parties and the odd theatre—and riding, of course."

I wasn't sure where her remarks tended. I said, "These occasions are nearly always a strain. You are picked out of ordinary life and dumped together after an elaborate ceremony—almost like two animals shut in a cage who haven't seen each other before."

"And now he sees me he doesn't like me."

"You are exaggerating."

"No." She added with anxiety, "I won't shock you, will I, if I tell you things? There's nobody else I can talk to."

"After fifty years I'm guaranteed shockproof."

"We haven't made love—properly, once, since we came here."

"What do you mean—properly?"

"He starts, but he doesn't finish; nothing happens."

I said uncomfortably, "Rochester wrote about that. A poem called 'The Imperfect Enjoyment.'" I don't know why I gave her this shady piece of literary information; perhaps, like a psychoanalyst, I wanted her not to feel alone with her problem. "It can happen to anybody."

"But it's not his fault," she said. "It's mine. I know it is. He just doesn't like my body."

"Surely it's a bit late to discover that."

"He'd never seen me naked till I came here," she said with the candour of a girl to her doctor—that was all I meant to her, I felt sure.

"There are nearly always first-night nerves. And then if a man worries (you must realize how much it hurts his pride) he can get stuck in the situation for days—

34

weeks even." I began to tell her about a mistress I once had—we stayed together a very long time and yet for two weeks at the beginning I could do nothing at all. "I was too anxious to succeed."

"That's different. You didn't hate the sight of her."

"You are making such a lot of so little."

"That's what he tries to do," she said with sudden school-girl coarseness and giggled miserably.

"We went away for a week and changed the scene, and everything after that was all right. For ten days it had been a flop, and for ten years afterwards we were happy. Very happy. But worry can get established in a room, in the colour of the curtains—it can hang itself up on coat-hangers; you find it smoking away in the ashtray marked Pernod, and when you look at the bed it pokes its head out from underneath like the toes of a pair of shoes." Again I repeated the only charm I could think of. "Take him home."

"It wouldn't make any difference. He's disappointed, that's all it is." She looked down at her long black legs; I followed the course of her eyes because I was finding now that I really wanted her and she said with sincere conviction, "I'm just not pretty enough when I'm undressed."

"You are talking real nonsense. You don't know what nonsense you are talking."

"Oh, no, I'm not. You see—it started all right, but then he touched me"—she put her hands on her breast—"and it all went wrong. I always knew they weren't much good. At school we used to have dormitory inspection—it was awful. Everybody could grow them

35

big except me. I'm no Jayne Mansfield, I can tell you."
She gave again that mirthless giggle. "I remember one
of the girls told me to sleep with a pillow on top—
she said they'd struggle for release and what they
needed was exercise. But of course it didn't work. I
doubt if the idea was very scientific." She added, "I
remember it was awfully hot at night like that."

"Peter doesn't strike me," I said cautiously, "as a man
who would want a Jayne Mansfield."

"But you understand, don't you, that, if he finds me
ugly, it's all so hopeless."

I wanted to agree with her—perhaps this reason
which she had thought up would be less distressing
than the truth, and soon enough there would be someone to cure her distrust. I had noticed before that it is
often the lovely women who have the least confidence
in their looks, but all the same I couldn't pretend to
her that I understood it her way. I said, "You must trust
me. There's nothing at all wrong with you and that's
why I'm talking to you the way I am."

"You are very sweet," she said, and her eyes passed
over me rather as the beam from the lighthouse which
at night went past the Musée Grimaldi and after a
certain time returned and brushed all our windows
indifferently on the hotel front. She continued, "He
said they'd be back by cocktail time."

"If you want a rest first"—for a little time we had
been close, but now again we were getting further and
further away. If I pressed her now she might in the
end be happy—does conventional morality demand
that a girl remain tied as she was tied? They'd been

married in church; she was probably a good Christian,
—and I know the ecclesiastical rules: at this moment of
her life she could be free of him, the marriage could be
annulled, but in a day or two it was only too probable
that the same rules would say, "He's managed well
enough, you are married for life."

And yet I couldn't press her. Wasn't I, after all, as-
suming far too much? Perhaps it was only a question
of first-night nerves; perhaps in a little while the three
of them would be back, silent, embarrassed, and Tony
in his turn would have a contusion on the cheek. I
would have been very glad to see it there; egotism
fades a little with the passions which engender it, and
I would have been content, I think, just to see her
happy.

So we returned to the hotel, not saying much, and
she went to her room and I to mine. It was in the end
a comedy and not a tragedy, a farce even, which is
why I have given this scrap of reminiscence a farcical
title.

VII

I was woken from my middle-aged siesta by the telephone. For a moment, surprised by the darkness, I
couldn't find the light switch. Scrambling for it, I
knocked over my bedside lamp; the telephone went on
ringing, and I tried to pick up the holder and knocked
over a tooth-glass in which I had given myself a whisky.
The little illuminated dial of my watch gleamed up at
me, marking eight-thirty. The telephone continued to

ring. I got the receiver off, but this time it was the ashtray which fell over. I couldn't get the cord to extend up to my ear, so I shouted in the direction of the telephone, "Hullo!"

A tiny sound came up from the floor which I interpreted as "Is that William?"

I shouted, "Hold on," and now that I was properly awake I realized the light switch was just over my head (in London it was placed over the bedside table). Little petulant noises came up from the floor as I put on the light, like the creaking of crickets.

"Who's that?" I said rather angrily, and then I recognized Tony's voice.

"William, whatever's the matter?"

"Nothing's the matter. Where are you?"

"But there was quite an enormous crash. It hurt my eardrum."

"An ashtray," I said.

"Do you usually hurl ashtrays around?"

"I was asleep."

"At eight-thirty? William! William!"

I said, "Where are you?"

"A little bar in what Mrs. Clarenty would call Monty."

"You promised to be back by dinner," I said.

"That's why I'm telephoning you. I'm being *responsible*, William. Do you mind telling Poopy that we'll be a little late? Give her dinner. Talk to her as only you know how. We'll be back by ten."

"Has there been an accident?"

I could hear him chuckling up the phone. "Oh, I wouldn't call it an accident."

38

"Why doesn't Peter call her himself?"

"He says he's not in the mood."

"But what shall I tell her—" The telephone went dead.

I got out of bed and dressed and then I called her room. She answered very quickly; I think she must have been sitting by the telephone. I relayed the message, asking her to meet me in the bar, and rang off before I had to face answering any questions.

But I found it was not so difficult as I feared to cover up; she was immensely relieved that somebody had telephoned. She had sat there in her room from half past seven onwards thinking of all the dangerous turns and ravines on the Grande Corniche, and when I rang she was half afraid that it might be the police or a hospital. Only after she had drunk two dry martinis and laughed quite a lot at her fears did she say, "I wonder why Tony rang you and not Peter me?"

I said (I had been working the answer out), "I gather he suddenly had an urgent appointment—in the loo."

It was as though I had said something enormously witty.

"Do you think they are a bit tight?" she asked.

"I wouldn't wonder."

"Darling Peter," she said. "He deserved the day off," and I couldn't help wondering in what direction his merit lay.

"Do you want another martini?"

"I'd better not," she said, "You've made me tight too."

I had become tired of the thin cold *rosé,* so we had a
bottle of real wine at dinner and she drank her full
share and talked about literature. She had, it seemed,
a nostalgia for Dornford Yates, had graduated in the
sixth form as far as Hugh Walpole, and now she talked
respectfully about Sir Charles Snow, who she obviously
thought had been knighted, like Sir Hugh, for his services to literature. I must have been deeply in love or
I would have found her innocence almost unbearable—
or perhaps I was a little tight as well. All the same, it
was to interrupt her flow of critical judgments that I
asked her what her real name was and she replied,
"Everyone calls me Poopy." I remembered the PT
stamped on her bags, but the only real names that I
could think of at the moment were Patricia and
Prunella. "Then I shall simply call you You," I said.

After dinner I had brandy and she had a kümmel. It
was past ten-thirty and still the three had not returned,
but she didn't seem to be worrying any more about
them. She sat on the floor of the bar beside me, and
every now and then the waiter looked in to see if he
could turn off the lights. She leant against me with her
hand on my knee and she said such things as "It must
be wonderful to be a writer," and in the glow of brandy
and tenderness I didn't mind them a bit. I even
began to tell her again about the Earl of Rochester.
What did I care about Dornford Yates, Hugh Walpole,
or Sir Charles Snow? I was even in the mood to recite
to her, hopelessly inapposite to the situation though
the lines were:

> Then talk not of Inconstancy,
>   False Hearts, and broken Vows;
> If I, by Miracle, can be
> This live-long Minute true to thee,
>   'Tis all that Heav'n allows

when the noise—what a noise—of the Sprite approaching brought us both to our feet. It was only too true that all that heaven allowed was the time in the bar at Antibes.

Tony was singing; we heard him all the way up the Boulevard Général Leclerc; Stephen was driving with the greatest caution, most of the time in second gear, and Peter, as we saw when we came out onto the terrace, was sitting on Tony's knee—nestling would be a better description—and joining in the refrain. All I could make out was

>   "Round and white
>   On a winter's night,
>   The hope of the Queen's Navee."

If they hadn't seen us on the steps I think they would have driven past the hotel without noticing.

"You *are* tight," the girl said with pleasure. Tony put his arm round her and ran her up to the top of the steps. "Be careful," she said, "William's made me tight, too."

"Good old William."

Stephen climbed carefully out of the car and sank down on the nearest chair.

"All well?" I asked, not knowing what I meant.

"The children have been very happy," he said, "and very, very relaxed."

"Got to go to the loo," Peter said (the cue was in the wrong place), and made for the stairs. The girl gave him a helping hand and I heard him say, "Wonderful day. Wonderful scenery. Wonderful . . ." She turned at the top of the stairs and swept us with her smile, gay, reassured, happy. As on the first night, when they had hesitated about the cocktail, they didn't come down again. There was a long silence and then Tony chuckled.

"You seem to have had a wonderful day," I said.

"Dear William, we've done a very good action. You've never seen him so *détendu.*"

Stephen sat saying nothing; I had the impression that today hadn't gone quite so well for him. Can people ever hunt quite equally in couples or is there always a loser? The too-grey waves of hair were as immaculate as ever, there was no contusion on the cheek, but I had the impression that the fear of the future had cast a long shadow.

"I suppose you mean you got him drunk?"

"Not with alcohol," Tony said. "We aren't vulgar seducers, are we, Stephen?" But Stephen made no reply.

"Then what was your good action?"

"*Le pauvre petit Pierre.* He was in such a state. He had quite convinced himself—or perhaps she had convinced him—that he was *impuissant.*"

"You seem to be making a lot of progress in French."

"It sounds more delicate in French."

"And with your help he found he wasn't?"

"After a little virginal timidity. Or near virginal.

42

School hadn't left him quite unmoved. Poor Poopy. She just hadn't known the right way to go about things. My dear, he has a superb virility. Where are you going, Stephen?"

"I'm going to bed," Stephen said flatly, and went up the steps alone. Tony looked after him, I thought with a kind of tender regret, a very light and superficial sorrow. "His rheumatism came back very badly this afternoon," he said. "Poor Stephen."

I thought it was well then to go to bed before I should become "Poor William" too. Tony's charity tonight was all-embracing.

VIII

It was the first morning for a long time that I found myself alone on the terrace for breakfast. The women in tweed skirts had been gone for some days, and I had never before known "the young men" to be absent. It was easy enough, while I waited for my coffee, to speculate about the likely reasons. There was, for example, the rheumatism . . . though I couldn't quite picture Tony in the character of a bedside companion. It was even remotely possible that they felt some shame and were unwilling to be confronted by their victim. As for the victim, I wondered sadly what painful revelation the night would certainly have brought. I blamed myself more than ever for not speaking in time. Surely she would have learned the truth more gently from me than from some tipsy uncontrolled outburst of her husband. All the same—such egoists are we in our passions—I was glad to be there in attendance . . . to staunch the tears . . . to take her tenderly in my arms, comfort her . . . oh, I had quite a romantic day-dream on the terrace before she came down the steps and I saw that she had never had less need of a comforter.

She was just as I had seen her the first night: shy, excited, gay, with a long and happy future established in her eyes. "William," she said, "can I sit at your table? Do you mind?"

"Of course not."

"You've been so patient with me all the time I was in the doldrums. I've talked an awful lot of nonsense to you. I know you told me it was nonsense, but I didn't believe you and you were right all the time."

I couldn't have interrupted her even if I had tried. She was a Venus at the prow sailing through sparkling seas. She said, "Everything's all right. Everything. Last night—he loves me, William. He really does. He's not a bit disappointed with me. He was just tired and strained, that's all. He needed a day off alone— *détendu*." She was even picking up Tony's French expressions second-hand. "I'm afraid of nothing now, nothing at all. Isn't it strange how black life seemed only two days ago? I really believe if it hadn't been for you I'd have thrown in my hand. How lucky I was to meet you and the others, too. They're such wonderful friends for Peter. We are all going home next week —and we've made a lovely plot together. Tony's going to come down almost immediately we get back and decorate our house. Yesterday, driving in the country, they had a wonderful discussion about it. You won't know our house when you see it—oh, I forgot, you never *have* seen it, have you? You must come down when it's all finished—with Stephen."

"Isn't Stephen going to help?" I just managed to slip in.

"Oh, he's too busy at the moment, Tony says, with Mrs. Clarenty. Do you like riding? Tony does. He adores horses, but he has so little chance in London. It will be wonderful for Peter—to have someone like that because, after all, I can't be riding with Peter all day long, there will be a lot of things to do in the house, especially now, when I'm not accustomed. It's wonderful to think that Peter won't have to be lonely. He says there are going to be Etruscan murals in the bathroom —whatever Etruscan means. The drawing-room *basically* will be eggshell green and the dining-room walls Pompeian red. They really did an awful lot of work yesterday afternoon—I mean in their heads, while we were glooming around. I said to Peter, 'As things are going now we'd better be prepared for a nursery,' but Peter said Tony was content to leave all that side to me. Then there are the stables: they were an old coach-house once, and Tony feels we could restore a lot of the ancient character, and there's a lamp he bought in St. Paul which will just fit. . . . It's endless the things there are to be done—a good six months' work, so Tony says, but luckily he can leave Mrs. Clarenty to Stephen and concentrate on us. Peter asked him about the garden, but he's not a specialist in gardens. He said, 'Everyone to his own *métier*,' and he's quite content if I bring in a man who knows all about roses.

"He knows Colin Winstanley too, of course, so there'll be quite a band of us. It's a pity the house won't be all ready for Christmas, but Peter says he's certain to have wonderful ideas for a really original tree. Peter thinks . . ."

She went on and on like that; perhaps I ought to have interrupted her even then; perhaps I should have tried to explain to her why her dream wouldn't last. Instead, I sat there silent, and presently I went to my room and packed—there was still one hotel open in the abandoned fun-fair of Juan between Maxim's and the boarded-up Strip Tease.

If I had stayed . . . who knows whether he could have kept on pretending for a second night? But I was just as bad for her as he was. If he had the wrong hormones, I had the wrong age. I didn't see any of them again before I left. She and Peter and Tony were out somewhere in the Sprite, and Stephen—so the receptionist told me —was lying late in bed with his rheumatism.

I planned a note for her, explaining rather feebly my departure, but when I came to write it I realized I had still no other name with which to address her than Poopy.

Beauty

The woman wore an orange scarf which she had so twisted around her forehead that it looked like a toque of the twenties, and her voice bulldozed through all opposition—the speech of her two companions, the young motorcyclist revving outside, even the clatter of soup plates in the kitchen of the small Antibes restaurant, which was almost empty now that autumn had truly set in. Her face was familiar to me; I had seen it looking down from the balcony of one of the reconditioned houses on the ramparts, while she called endearments to someone or something invisible below. But I hadn't seen her since the summer sun had gone, and I thought she had departed with the other foreigners. She said, "I'll be in Vienna for Christmas. I just love it there. Those lovely white horses—and the little boys singing Bach."

Her companions were English; the man was struggling still to maintain the appearance of a summer visitor, but he shivered in secret every now and then in his blue cotton sports shirt. He asked throatily, "We won't see you then in London?" and his wife, who was much younger than either of them, said, "Oh, but you simply must come."

"There are difficulties," she said. "But if you two dear people are going to be in Venice in the spring . . ."

"I don't suppose we'll have enough money, will we, darling, but we'd love to show you London. Wouldn't we, darling?"

"Of course," he said gloomily.

"I'm afraid that's quite, quite impossible, because of Beauty, you see."

I hadn't noticed Beauty until then because he was so well-behaved. He lay flat on the window-sill as inert as a cream bun on a counter. I think he was the most perfect Pekingese I have ever seen—although I can't pretend to know the points a judge ought to look for. He would have been as white as milk if a little coffee had not been added, but that was hardly an imperfection—it enhanced his beauty. His eyes from where I sat seemed deep black, like the centre of a flower, and they were completely undisturbed by thought. This was not a dog to respond to the word "rat" or to show a youthful enthusiasm if someone suggested a walk. Nothing less than his own image in a glass would rouse him, I imagined, to a flicker of interest. He was certainly well fed enough to ignore the meal that the others had left unfinished, though perhaps he was accustomed to something richer than langouste.

"You couldn't leave him with a friend?" the younger woman asked.

"Leave Beauty?" The question didn't rate a reply. She ran her fingers through the long *café-au-lait* hair, but the dog made no motion with his tail as a common dog might have done. He gave a kind of grunt like an old man in a club who has been disturbed by the waiter. "All these laws of quarantine—why don't your congressmen do something about them?"

"We call them MP's," the man said with what I thought was hidden dislike.

"I don't care what you call them. They live in the Middle Ages. I can go to Paris, to Vienna, Venice— why, I could go to Moscow if I wanted, but I can't go to London without leaving Beauty in a horrible prison. With all kinds of undesirable dogs."

"I think he'd have—" he hesitated with what I thought was admirable English courtesy as he weighed in the balance the correct term—cell? kennel?—"a room of his own."

"Think of the diseases he might pick up." She lifted him from the window-sill as easily as she might have lifted a stole of fur and pressed him resolutely against her left breast; he didn't even grunt. I had the sense of something completely possessed. A child at least would have rebelled . . . for a time. Poor child. I don't know why I couldn't pity the dog. Perhaps he was too beautiful.

She said, "Poor Beauty's thirsty."

"I'll get him some water," the man said.

"A half-bottle of Evian, if you don't mind. I don't trust the tap-water."

It was then that I left them, because the cinema in the Place de Gaulle opened at nine.

It was after eleven that I emerged again, and, since the night was fine, except for a cold wind off the Alps, I made a circuit from the Place and, as the ramparts would be too exposed, I took the narrow dirty streets off the Place Nationale—in the rue de Sade, the rue des Bains . . . The dustbins were all out and dogs had made ordure on the pavements and children had urinated in the gutters. A patch of white, which I first took to be a cat, moved stealthily along the house-fronts ahead of me, then paused, and as I approached snaked behind a dustbin. I stood amazed and watched. A pattern of light through the slats of a shutter striped the road in yellow tigerish bars, and presently Beauty slid out again and looked at me with his pansy face and black expressionless eyes. I think he expected me to lift him up, and he showed his teeth in warning.

"Why, Beauty!" I exclaimed. He gave his clubman grunt again and waited. Was he cautious because he found that I knew his name or did he recognize in my clothes and my smell that I belonged to the same class as the woman in the toque, that I was one who would disapprove of his nocturnal ramble? Suddenly he cocked an ear in the direction of the house on the ramparts; it was possible that he had heard a woman's voice calling. Certainly he looked dubiously up at me as though he wanted to see whether I had heard it too, and perhaps because I made no move he considered he was safe. He began to undulate down the pavement with a purpose, like the feather boa in the cabaret act which floats around seeking a top-hat. I followed at a discreet distance.

Was it memory or a keen sense of smell which affected him? Of all the dustbins in the mean street there was only one which had lost its cover—indescribable tendrils drooped over the top. Beauty—he ignored me as completely now as he would have ignored an inferior dog—stood on his hind legs with two delicately feathered paws holding the edge of the bin. He turned his head and looked at me, without expression, two pools of ink in which a soothsayer perhaps could have read an infinite series of predictions. He gave a scramble like an athlete raising himself on a parallel bar, and he was within the dustbin, and the feathered forepaws—I am sure I have read somewhere that the feathering is very important in a contest of Pekingese—were rooting and delving among the old vegetables, the empty cartons, the squashy fragments in the bin. He became excited and his nose went down like a pig after truffles. Then his back paws got into play, discarding the rubbish behind—old fruit-skins fell on the pavement and rotten figs, fish-heads. . . . At last he had what he had come for—a long tube of intestine belonging to God knows what animal; he tossed it in the air, so that it curled round the milk-white throat. Then he abandoned the dustbin, and he galumphed down the street like a harlequin, trailing behind him the intestine, which might have been a string of sausages.

I must admit I was wholly on his side. Surely anything was better than the embrace of a flat breast.

Round a turning he found a dark corner obviously more suited than all the others to gnawing an intestine because it contained a great splash of ordure. He tested the ordure first, like the clubman he was, with his nostrils, and then he rolled lavishly back on it, paws in the air, rubbing the *café-au-lait* fur in the dark shampoo, the intestines trailing from his mouth, while the satin eyes gazed imperturbably up at the great black Midi sky.

Curiosity took me back home, after all, by way of the ramparts, and there over the balcony the woman leant, trying, I suppose, to detect her dog in the shadows of the street below. "Beauty!" I heard her call wearily, "Beauty!" And then with growing impatience, "Beauty! Come home! You've done your wee-wee, Beauty. Where are you, Beauty, Beauty?" Such small things ruin our sense of compassion, for surely, if it had not been for that hideous orange toque, I would have felt some pity for the old sterile thing, perched up there, calling for lost Beauty.

Chagrin in Three Parts

I

It was February in Antibes. Gusts of rain blew along the
ramparts, and the emaciated statues on the terrace of
the Château Grimaldi dripped with wet, and there was
a sound absent during the flat blue days of summer, the
continual rustle below the ramparts of the small surf.
All along the Côte the summer restaurants were closed,
but lights shone in Félix au Port and one Peugeot of the
latest model stood in the parking-rank. The bare masts
of the abandoned yachts stuck up like toothpicks and the
last plane in the winter service dropped, in a flicker of
green, red, and yellow lights, like Christmas-tree bau-
bles, towards the airport of Nice. This was the Antibes I
always enjoyed; and I was disappointed to find I was not
alone in the restaurant as I was most nights of the week.
Crossing the road I saw a very powerful lady dressed
in black who stared out at me from one of the window
tables, as though she were willing me not to enter, and
when I came in and took my place before the other win-

dow she regarded me with too evident distaste. My
raincoat was shabby and my shoes were muddy, and in
any case I was a man. Momentarily, while she took me
in, from balding top to shabby toe, she interrupted her
conversation with the *patronne,* who addressed her as
Madame Dejoie.

Madame Dejoie continued her monologue in a tone of
firm disapproval: it was unusual for Madame Volet to be
late, but she hoped nothing had happened to her on the
ramparts. In winter there were always Algerians about,
she added with mysterious apprehension, as though she
were talking of wolves, but none the less Madame Volet
had refused Madame Dejoie's offer to be fetched from
her home. "I did not press her under the circumstances.
Poor Madame Volet." Her hand clutched a huge pepper-
mill like a bludgeon, and I pictured Madame Volet as a
weak timid old lady, dressed too in black, afraid even
of protection by so formidable a friend.

How wrong I was. Madame Volet blew suddenly in
with a gust of rain through the side door beside my
table, and she was young and extravagantly pretty, in
her tight black pants, and with a long neck emerging
from a wine-red polo-necked sweater. I was glad when
she sat down side by side with Madame Dejoie, so that
I need not lose the sight of her while I ate.

"I am late," she said. "I know that I am late. So many
little things have to be done when you are alone, and I
am not yet accustomed to being alone," she added with
a pretty little sob which reminded me of a cut-glass Vic-
torian tear-bottle. She took off thick winter gloves with
a wringing gesture which made me think of handker-

chiefs wet with grief, and her hands looked suddenly small and useless and vulnerable.

"*Pauvre cocotte,*" said Madame Dejoie, "be quiet here with me and forget awhile. I have ordered a bouillabaisse with langouste."

"But I have no appetite, Emmy."

"It will come back. You'll see. Now here is your porto and I have ordered a bottle of *blanc de blancs.*"

"You will make me *tout à fait soûle.*"

"We are going to eat and drink, and for a little while we are both going to forget everything. I know exactly how you are feeling, for I too lost a beloved husband."

"By death," little Madame Volet said. "That makes a great difference. Death is quite bearable."

"It is more irrevocable."

"Nothing can be more irrevocable than my situation. Emmy, he loves the little bitch."

"All I know of her is that she has deplorable taste— or a deplorable hairdresser."

"But that was exactly what I told him."

"You were wrong. I should have told him, not you, for he might have believed me, and in any case my criticism would not have hurt his pride."

"I love him," Madame Volet said, "I cannot be prudent," and then she suddenly became aware of my presence. She whispered something to her companion, and I heard the reassurance, "*Un anglais.*" I watched her as covertly as I could—like most writers I have the spirit of a *voyeur*—and I wondered how stupid married men could be. I was temporarily free, and I very much wanted to console her, but I didn't exist in her eyes, now she knew that I was English, nor in the eyes of Madame Dejoie. I was less than human—I was only a reject from the Common Market.

I ordered two small *rougets* and a half bottle of Pouilly and I tried to be interested in the Trollope I had brought with me. But my attention strayed.

"I adored my husband," Madame Dejoie was saying, and her hand again grasped the pepper-mill, but this time it looked less like a bludgeon.

"I still do, Emmy. That is the worst of it. I know that if he came back . . ."

"Mine can never come back," Madame Dejoie retorted, touching the corner of one eye with her handkerchief and then examining the smear of black left behind.

In a gloomy silence they both drained their portos. Then Madame Dejoie said with determination, "There is no turning back. You should accept that as I do. There remains for us only the problem of adaptation."

"After such a betrayal I could never look at another man," Madame Volet replied. At that moment she looked right through me. I felt invisible. I put my hand between the light and the wall to prove that I had a shadow, and the shadow looked like a beast with horns.

"I would never suggest another man," Madame Dejoie said. "Never."

"What then?"

"When my poor husband died from an infection of the bowels I thought myself quite inconsolable, but I said to myself, Courage, courage. You must learn to laugh again."

56

"To laugh!" Madame Volet exclaimed. "To laugh at what?" But before Madame Dejoie could reply, Monsieur Félix had arrived to perform his neat surgical operation upon the fish for the bouillabaisse. Madame Dejoie watched with real interest; Madame Volet, I thought, watched for politeness' sake while she finished a glass of *blanc de blancs*.

When the operation was over Madame Dejoie filled the glasses and said, "I was lucky enough to have *une amie* who taught me not to mourn for the past." She raised her glass and, cocking a finger as I had seen men do, she added, *"Pas de mollesse."*

"Pas de mollesse," Madame Volet repeated with a wan enchanting smile.

I felt decidedly ashamed of myself—a cold literary observer of human anguish. I was afraid of catching poor Madame Volet's eyes (what kind of a man was capable of betraying her for a woman who took the wrong sort of rinse?) and I tried to occupy myself with sad Mr. Crawley's courtship as he stumped up the muddy lane in his big clergyman's boots. In any case, the two of them had dropped their voices; a gentle smell of garlic came to me from the bouillabaisse, the bottle of *blanc de blancs* was nearly finished, and, in spite of Madame Volet's protestation, Madame Dejoie had called for another. "There are no half bottles," she said. "We can always leave something for the gods." Again their voices sank to an intimate murmur as Mr. Crawley's suit was accepted (though how he was to support an inevitably large family would not appear until the succeeding volume). I was startled out of my forced concentration by a laugh: a musical laugh: it was Madame Volet's.

"*Cochon!*" she exclaimed.

Madame Dejoie regarded her over her glass (the new bottle had already been broached) under beetling brows. "I am telling you the truth," she said. "He would crow like a cock."

"But what a joke to play!"

"It began as a joke, but he was really proud of himself. *Aprés seulement deux coups . . .*"

"*Jamais trois?*" Madame Volet asked and she giggled and splashed a little of her wine down her polo-necked collar.

"*Jamais.*"

"*Je suis saoule.*"

"*Moi aussi, cocotte.*"

Madame Volet said, "To crow like a cock—at least it was a *fantaisie*. My husband has no *fantaisies*. He is strictly classical."

"*Pas de vices?*"

"*Hélas, pas de vices.*"

"And yet you miss him?"

"He worked hard," Madame Volet said and giggled. "To think that at the end he must have been working hard for both of us."

"You found it a little boring?"

"It was a habit—how one misses a habit. I wake now at five in the morning."

"At five?"

"It was the hour of his greatest activity."

"My husband was a very small man," Madame Dejoie

said. "Not in height, of course. He was two meters high."

"Oh, Paul is big enough—but always the same."

"Why do you continue to love that man?" Madame Dejoie sighed and put her large hand on Madame Volet's knee. She wore a signet ring which perhaps had belonged to her late husband. Madame Volet sighed too, and I thought melancholy was returning to the table, but then she hiccupped and both of them laughed.

"Tu es vraiment saoule, cocotte."

"Do I truly miss Paul, or is it only that I miss his habits?" She suddenly met my eye and blushed right down into the wine-coloured wine-stained polo-necked collar.

Madame Dejoie repeated reassuringly, *"Un anglais— ou un américain."* She hardly bothered to lower her voice at all. "Do you know how limited my experience was when my husband died? I loved him when he crowed like a cock. I was glad he was so pleased. I only wanted him to be pleased. I adored him, and yet in those days—*j'ai joui peut-être trois fois par semaine.* I did not expect more. It seemed to me a natural limit."

"In my case it was three times a day," Madame Volet said and giggled again. *"Mais toujours d'une façon classique."* She put her hands over her face and gave a little sob. Madame Dejoie put an arm round her shoulders. There was a long silence while the remains of the bouillabaisse were cleared away.

II

"Men are curious animals," Madame Dejoie said at last. The coffee had come and they divided one *marc* between them, in turn dipping lumps of sugar which they inserted into each other's mouth. "Animals too lack imagination. A dog has no *fantaisie*."

"How bored I have been sometimes," Madame Volet said. "He would talk politics continually and turn on the news at eight in the morning. At eight! What do I care for politics? But if I asked his advice about anything important he showed no interest at all. With you I can talk about anything, about the whole world."

"I adored my husband," Madame Dejoie said, "yet it was only after his death I discovered my capacity for love. With Pauline. You never knew Pauline. She died five years ago. I loved her more than I ever loved Jacques, and yet I felt no despair when she died. I knew that it was not the end, for I knew by then my capacity."

"I have never loved a woman," Madame Volet said.

"*Chérie*, then you do not know what love can mean. With a woman you do not have to be content with *une façon classique* three times a day."

"I love Paul, but he is different from me in every way . . ."

"Unlike Pauline, he is a man."

"Oh Emmy, you describe him so perfectly. How well you understand. A man!"

"When you really think of it, how comic that little object is. Hardly enough to crow about, one would think."

60

Madame Volet giggled and said, "*Cochon.*"

"Perhaps smoked like an eel one might enjoy it."

"Stop it. Stop it." They rocked up and down with little gusts of laughter. They were drunk, of course, but in the most charming way.

III

How distant now seemed Trollope's muddy lane, the heavy boots of Mr. Crawley, his proud shy courtship. In time we travel a space as vast as any astronaut's. When I looked up Madame Volet's head rested on Madame Dejoie's shoulder. "I feel so sleepy," she said.

"Tonight you shall sleep, *chérie.*"

"I am so little good to you. I know nothing."

"In love one learns quickly."

"But am I in love?" Madame Volet asked, sitting up very straight and staring into Madame Dejoie's sombre eyes.

"If the answer were no, you wouldn't ask the question."

"But I thought I could never love again."

"Not another man," Madame Dejoie said. "*Chérie,* you are almost asleep. Come."

"The bill?" Madame Volet said as though perhaps she were trying to delay the moment of decision.

"I will pay tomorrow. What a pretty coat this is—but not warm enough, *chérie,* in February. You need to be cared for."

"You have given me back my courage," Madame Volet said. "When I came in here I was *si démoralisée.* . . ."

"Soon—I promise—you will be able to laugh at the past. . . ."

"I have already laughed," Madame Volet said. "Did he really crow like a cock?"

"Yes."

"I shall never be able to forget what you said about smoked eel. Never. If I saw one now . . ." She began to giggle again and Madame Dejoie steadied her a little on the way to the door.

I watched them cross the road to the car-park. Suddenly Madame Volet gave a little hop and skip and flung her arms around Madame Dejoie's neck, and the wind, blowing through the archway of the port, carried the faint sound of her laughter to me where I sat alone *chez* Félix. I was glad she was happy again. I was glad that she was in the kind reliable hands of Madame Dejoie. What a fool Paul had been, I reflected, feeling *chagrin* myself now for so many wasted opportunities.

The Over-night Bag

The little man who came to the information desk in Nice airport when they demanded "Henry Cooper, passenger on BEA flight 105 for London" looked like a shadow cast by the brilliant glitter of the sun. He wore a grey town-suit and black shoes; he had a grey skin which carefully matched his suit, and, since it was impossible for him to change his skin, it was possible that he had no other suit.

"Are you Mr. Cooper?"

"Yes." He carried a BOAC over-night bag and he laid it tenderly on the ledge of the information desk as though it contained something precious and fragile like an electric razor.

"There is a telegram for you."

He opened it and read the message twice over. "Bon voyage. Much missed. You will be welcome home, dear boy. Mother." He tore the telegram once across and left it on the desk, from which the girl in the blue uniform, after a discreet interval, picked the pieces and with natural curiosity joined them together. Then she looked for the little grey man among the passengers who were now lining up at the tourist gate to join the Trident. He was among the last, carrying his blue BOAC bag.

Near the front of the plane Henry Cooper found a window-seat and placed the bag on the central seat beside him. A large woman in pale blue trousers too tight for the size of her buttocks took the third seat. She squeezed a very large handbag in beside the other on the central seat, and she laid a large fur coat on top of both. Henry Cooper said, "May I put it on the rack, please?"

She looked at him with contempt. "Put what?"

"Your coat."

"If you want to. Why?"

"It's a very heavy coat. It's squashing my over-night bag."

He was so small he could stand nearly upright under the rack. When he sat down he fastened the seat-belt over the two bags before he fastened his own. The woman watched him with suspicion. "I've never seen anyone do that before," she said.

"I don't want it shaken about," he said. "There are storms over London."

"You haven't got an animal in there, have you?"

"Not exactly."

"It's cruel to carry an animal shut up like that," she said, as though she disbelieved him.

As the Trident began its run he laid his hand on the

bag as if he were reassuring something within. The
woman watched the bag narrowly. If she saw the least
movement of life she had made up her mind to call the
stewardess. Even if it were only a tortoise . . . A tortoise needed air, or so she supposed, in spite of hiber-
nation. When they were safely airborne he relaxed and
began to read a *Nice-Matin*—he spent a good deal of
time on each story as though his French were not very
good. The woman struggled angrily to get her big cavernous bag from under the seat-belt. She muttered
"Ridiculous" twice for his benefit. Then she made up,
put on thick horn-rimmed glasses and began to reread a
letter which began "My darling Tiny" and ended "Your
own cuddly Bertha." After a while she grew tired of the
weight on her knees and dropped it onto the BOAC
over-night bag.

The little man leapt in distress. "Please," he said,
"please." He lifted her bag and pushed it quite rudely
into a corner of the seat. "I don't want it squashed," he
said. "It's a matter of respect."

"What have you got in your precious bag?" she asked
him angrily.

"A dead baby," he said. "I thought I had told you."

"On the left of the aircraft," the pilot announced
through the loudspeaker, "you will see Montélimar. We
shall be passing Paris in . . ."

"You are not serious," she said.

"It's just one of those things," he replied in a tone that
carried conviction.

"But you can't take dead babies—like that—in a bag
—in the economy class."

"In the case of a baby it is so much cheaper than freight. Only a week old. It weighs so little."

"But it should be in a coffin, not an over-night bag."

"My wife didn't trust a foreign coffin. She said the materials they use are not durable. She's rather a conventional woman."

"Then it's *your* baby?" Under the circumstances she seemed almost prepared to sympathize.

"My wife's baby," he corrected her.

"What's the difference?"

He said sadly, "There could well be a difference." And turned the page of *Nice-Matin*.

"Are you suggesting . . ." But he was deep in a column dealing with a Lions Club meeting in Antibes and the rather revolutionary suggestion made there by a member from Grasse. She read over again her letter from "cuddly Bertha," but it failed to hold her attention. She kept on stealing a glance at the over-night bag.

"You don't anticipate trouble with the customs?" she asked him after a while.

"Of course I shall have to declare it," he said. "It was acquired abroad."

When they landed, exactly on time, he said to her with old-fashioned politeness, "I have enjoyed our flight." She looked for him with a certain morbid curiosity in the customs—Channel 10—but then she saw him in Channel 12, for passengers carrying hand-baggage only. He was speaking, earnestly, to the officer who was poised, chalk in hand, over the over-night bag. Then she lost sight of him as her own inspector insisted on examining the contents of her cavernous bag, which yielded up a number of undeclared presents for Bertha.

Henry Cooper was the first out of the arrivals door and he took a hired car. The charge for taxis rose every year when he went abroad and it was his one extravagance not to wait for the airport-bus. The sky was overcast and the temperature only a little above freezing, but the driver was in a mood of euphoria. He had a dashing comradely air—he told Henry Cooper that he had won fifty pounds on the pools. The heater was on full blast, and Henry Cooper opened the window, but an icy current of air from Scandinavia flowed round his shoulders. He closed the window again and said, "Would you mind turning off the heater?" It was as hot in the car as in a New York hotel during a blizzard.

"It's cold outside," the driver said.

"You see," Henry Cooper said, "I have a dead baby in my bag."

"Dead baby?"

"Yes."

"Ah, well," the driver said, "he won't feel the heat, will he? It's a he?"

"Yes. A he. I'm anxious he shouldn't—deteriorate."

"They keep a long time," the driver said. "You'd be surprised. Longer than old people. What did you have for lunch?"

Henry Cooper was a little surprised. He had to cast his mind back. He said, *"Carré d'agneau à la provençale."*

"Curry?"

"No, not curry, lamb chops with garlic and herbs. And then an apple tart."

"And you drank something, I wouldn't be surprised."

"A half bottle of *rosé*. And a brandy."

"There you are, you see."

"I don't understand."

"With all that inside you, you wouldn't keep so well."

Gillette Razors were half hidden in icy mist. The driver had forgotten or had refused to turn down the heat, but he remained silent for quite a while, perhaps brooding on the subject of life and death.

"How did the little perisher die?" he asked at last.

"They die so easily," Henry Cooper answered.

"Many a true word's spoken in jest," the driver said, a little absent-mindedly because he had swerved to avoid a car which braked too suddenly, and Henry Cooper instinctively put his hand on the over-night bag to steady it.

"Sorry," the driver said. "Not my fault. Amateur drivers! Anyway, you don't need to worry—they can't bruise after death, or can they? I read something about it once in *The Cases of Sir Bernard Spilsbury,* but I don't remember now exactly what. That's always the trouble about reading."

"I'd be much happier," Henry Cooper said, "if you would turn off the heat."

"There's no point in you catching a chill, is there? Or me either. It won't help *him* where he's gone—if anywhere at all. The next thing you know you'll be in the same position yourself. Not in an over-night bag, of course. That goes without saying."

The Knightsbridge tunnel as usual was closed because of flooding. They turned north through the park. The trees dripped on empty branches. The pigeons blew out their grey feathers the colour of soiled city snow.

"Is he yours?" the driver asked. "If you don't mind my inquiring?"

"Not exactly." Henry Cooper added briskly and brightly, "My wife's, as it happens."

"It's never the same if it's not your own," the driver said thoughtfully. "I had a nephew who died. He had a split palate—that wasn't the reason, of course, but it made it easier to bear for the parents. Are you going to an undertaker's now?"

"I thought I would take it home for the night and see about the arrangements tomorrow."

"A little perisher like that would fit easily into the fridge. No bigger than a chicken. As a precaution only."

They entered the large whitewashed Bayswater square. The houses resembled the above-ground tombs you find in Continental cemeteries, except that, unlike the tombs, they were divided into flatlets and there were rows and rows of bell-pushes to wake the inmates. The driver watched Henry Cooper get out with the over-night bag at a portico entitled Stare House. "Bloody orful aircraft company," he said mechanically when he saw the letters BOAC—without ill-will, it was only a Pavlov response.

Henry Cooper went up to the top floor and let himself in. His mother was already in the hall to greet him. "I saw your car draw up, dear." He put the over-night bag on a chair so as to embrace her better.

"You've come quickly. You got my telegram at Nice?"

"Yes, mother. With only an over-night bag I walked straight through the customs."

"So clever of you to travel light."

"It's the drip-dry shirt that does it," Henry Cooper said. He followed his mother into their sitting-room. He noticed she had changed the position of his favourite picture—a reproduction from *Life* magazine of a painting by Hieronymus Bosch. "Just so that I don't see it from *my* chair, dear," his mother explained, interpreting his glance. His slippers were laid out by his armchair and he sat down with an air of satisfaction at being home again.

"And now, dear," his mother said, "tell me how it was. Tell me everything. Did you make some new friends?"

"Oh, yes, Mother, wherever I went I made friends." Winter had fallen early on the House of Stare. The over-night bag disappeared in the darkness of the hall like a blue fish into blue water.

"And adventures? What adventures?"

Once, while he talked, his mother got up and tiptoed to draw the curtains and to turn on a reading-lamp, and once she gave a little gasp of horror. "A little toe? In the marmalade?"

"Yes, Mother."

"It wasn't English marmalade?"

"No, Mother, foreign."

"I could have understood a finger—an accident slicing the oranges—but a toe!"

"As I understand it," Henry Cooper said, "in those

parts they use a kind of guillotine worked by the bare foot of a peasant."

"You complained, of course?"

"Not in words, but I put the toe very conspicuously at the edge of the plate."

After one more story it was time for his mother to go and put the shepherd's pie into the oven, and Henry Cooper went into the hall to fetch the over-night bag. "Time to unpack," he thought. He had a tidy mind.

Mortmain

How wonderfully secure and peaceful a genuine marriage seemed to Carter, when he attained it at the age of forty-two. He even enjoyed every moment of the church service, except when he saw Josephine wiping away a tear as he conducted Julia down the aisle. It was typical of this new frank relationship that Josephine was there at all. He had no secrets from Julia; they had often talked together of his ten tormented years with Josephine, of her extravagant jealousy, of her well-timed hysterics. "It was her insecurity," Julia argued with understanding, and she was quite convinced that in a little while it would be possible to form a friendship with Josephine.

"I doubt it, darling."

"Why? I can't help being fond of anyone who loved you."

"It was a rather cruel love."

"Perhaps at the end when she knew she was losing you, but, darling, there *were* happy years."

"Yes." But he wanted to forget that he had ever loved anyone before Julia.

Her generosity sometimes staggered him. On the seventh day of their honeymoon, when they were drinking retsina in a little restaurant on the beach by Sunium, he accidentally took a letter from Josephine out of his pocket. It had arrived the day before and he had concealed it, for fear of hurting Julia. It was typical of Josephine that she could not leave him alone for the brief period of the honeymoon. Even her handwriting was now abhorrent to him—very neat, very small, in black ink the colour of her hair. Julia was platinum-fair. How had he ever thought that black hair was beautiful? Or been impatient to read letters in black ink?

"What's the letter, darling? I didn't know there had been a post."

"It's from Josephine. It came yesterday."

"But you haven't even opened it!" she exclaimed without a word of reproach.

"I don't want to think about her."

"But darling, she may be ill."

"Not she."

"Or in distress."

"She earns more with her fashion-designs than I do with my stories."

"Darling, let's be kind. We can afford to be. We are so happy."

So he opened the letter. It was affectionate and uncomplaining and he read it with distaste.

Dear Philip,

I didn't want to be a death's head at the reception, so I had no chance to say goodbye and wish you both the greatest possible happiness. I thought Julia looked terribly beautiful and so very, very young. You must look after her carefully. I know how well you can do that, Philip dear. When I saw her, I couldn't help wondering why you took such a long time to make up your mind to leave me. Silly Philip. It's much less painful to act quickly.

I don't suppose you are interested to hear about my activities now, but just in case you are worrying a little about me—you know what an old worrier you are—I want you to know that I'm working *very* hard at a whole series for—guess—the French *Vogue*. They are paying me a fortune in francs, and I simply have no time for unhappy thoughts. I've been back once—I hope you don't mind—to our apartment (slip of the tongue) because I'd lost a key sketch. I found it at the back of our communal drawer—the ideas-bank, do you remember? I thought I'd taken all my stuff away, but there it was between the leaves of the story you started that heavenly summer, and never finished, at Napoule. Now I'm rambling on when all I really wanted to say was: Be happy both of you.

Love, Josephine

Carter handed the letter to Julia and said, "It could have been worse."

"But would she like me to read it?"

"Oh, it's meant for both of us." Again he thought how wonderful it was to have no secrets. There had been so many secrets during the last ten years, even innocent secrets, for fear of misunderstanding, of Josephine's rage or silence. Now he had no fear of anything at all: he could have trusted even a guilty secret to Julia's sympathy and comprehension. He said, "I was a fool not to show you the letter yesterday. I'll never do anything like that again." He tried to recall Spenser's line —"Port after stormie seas."

When Julia had finished reading the letter she said, "I think she's a wonderful woman. How very, very sweet of her to write like that. You know I was—only now and then, of course—just a little bit worried about her. After all *I* wouldn't like to lose you after ten years."

When they were in the taxi going back to Athens she said, "Were you very happy at Napoule?"

"Yes, I suppose so. I don't remember. It wasn't like this."

With the antennae of a lover he could feel her moving away from him, though their shoulders still touched. The sun was bright on the road from Sunium, the warm sleepy loving siesta lay ahead, and yet . . . "Is anything the matter, darling?" he asked.

"Not really . . . It's only . . . do you think one day you'll say the same about Athens as about Napoule? 'I don't remember, it wasn't like this.' "

"What a dear fool you are," he said, and kissed her. After that they played a little in the taxi going back to Athens, and when the streets began to unroll she sat up and combed her hair. "You aren't really a cold man, are you?" she asked, and he knew that all was right again.

It was Josephine's fault that—momentarily—there had been a small division.

When they got out of bed to have dinner, she said, "We must write to Josephine."

"Oh, no!"

"Darling, I know how you feel, but really it was a wonderful letter."

"A picture-postcard then."

So they agreed on that.

Suddenly it was autumn when they arrived back in London—if not winter already, for there was ice in the rain falling on the tarmac, and they had quite forgotten how early the lights came on at home—passing Gillette and Lucozade and Smith's Crisps, and no view of the Parthenon anywhere. The BOAC posters seemed more than usually sad—"BOAC takes you there and brings you back."

"We'll put on all the electric fires as soon as we get in," Carter said, "and it will be warm in no time at all." But when they opened the door of the apartment they found the fires were already alight. Little glows greeted them in the twilight from the depths of the living-room and the bedroom.

"Some fairy has done this," Julia said.

"Not a fairy of any kind," Carter said. He had already seen the envelope on the mantlepiece addressed in black ink to "Mrs. Carter."

Dear Julia, you won't mind my calling you Julia, will you? I feel we have so much in common, having loved the same man. Today was so icy-cold that I could not help thinking of how you two were returning from the sun and the warmth to a cold flat. (I know how cold the flat can be. I used to catch a chill every year when we came back from the south of France.) So I've done a very presumptuous thing. I've slipped in and put on the fires, but to show you that I'll never do such a thing again, I've hidden my key under the mat outside the front door. That's just in case your plane is held up in Rome or somewhere. I'll telephone the airport and if by some unlikely chance you haven't arrived, I'll come back and turn out the fires for safety (and economy! the rates are awful). Wishing you a very warm evening in your new home, love from Josephine.

P.S. I did notice that the coffee jar was empty, so I've left a packet of Blue Mountain in the kitchen. It's the only coffee Philip really cares for.

"Well," Julia said laughing, "she does think of everything."

"I wish she'd just leave us alone," Carter said.

"We wouldn't be warm like this, and we wouldn't have any coffee for breakfast."

"I feel that she's lurking about the place and she'll walk in at any moment. Just when I'm kissing you." He kissed Julia with one careful eye on the door.

"You *are* a bit unfair, darling. After all, she's left her key under the mat."

"She might have had a duplicate made."

She closed his mouth with another kiss.

"Have you noticed how erotic an aeroplane makes you after a few hours?" Carter asked.

"Yes."

"I suppose it's the vibration."

"Let's do something about it, darling."

"I'll just look under the mat first. To make sure she wasn't lying."

He enjoyed marriage—so much that he blamed himself for not having married before, forgetting that in that case he would have been married to Josephine. He found Julia, who had no work of her own, almost miraculously available. There was no maid to mar their relationship with habits. As they were always together, at cocktail parties, in restaurants, at small dinner parties, they had only to meet each other's eyes . . . Julia soon earned the reputation of being delicate and easily tired; it occurred so often that they left a cocktail party after a quarter of an hour or abandoned a dinner after the coffee—"Oh dear, I'm so sorry, such a vile headache, so stupid of me. Philip, *you* must stay. . . ."

"Of course I'm not going to stay."

Once they had a narrow escape from discovery on the stairs while they were laughing uncontrollably. Their host had followed them out to ask them to post a letter. Julia in the nick of time changed her laughter into what seemed to be a fit of hysterics. . . . Several weeks went by. It was a really successful marriage. . . . They liked—between whiles—to discuss its success, each attributing the main merit to the other. "When I think you might have married Josephine," Julia said. "Why didn't you marry Josephine?"

"I suppose at the back of our minds we knew it wasn't going to be permanent."

"Are we going to be permanent?"

"If we aren't, nothing will ever be."

It was early in November that the time-bombs began to go off. No doubt they had been planned to explode earlier, but Josephine had not taken into account the temporary change in his habits. Some weeks passed before he had occasion to open what they used to call the ideas-bank in the days of their closest companionship—the drawer in which he used to leave notes for stories, scraps of overheard dialogue, and the like, and she would leave roughly sketched ideas for fashion advertisements.

Directly he opened the drawer he saw her letter. It was labelled heavily "Top Secret" in black ink with a whimsically drawn exclamation mark in the form of a girl with big eyes (Josephine suffered in an elegant way from exophthalmic goitre) rising genie-like out of a bottle. He read the letter with extreme distaste:

> Dear, you didn't expect to find me here, did you? But after ten years I can't not now and then say, Good night or Good morning, how are you? Bless you. Lots of love (really and truly), Your Josephine.

The threat of "now and then" was unmistakable. He slammed the drawer shut and said "Damn" so loudly that Julia looked in.

"Whatever is it, darling?"

"Josephine again."

She read the letter and said, "You know, I can understand the way she feels. Poor Josephine. Are you tearing it up, darling?"

"What else do you expect me to do with it? Keep it for a collected edition of her letters?"

"It just seems a bit unkind."

"Me unkind to *her?* Julia, you've no idea of the sort of life that we led those last years. I can show you scars. When she was in a rage she would stub her cigarettes *anywhere.*"

"She felt she was losing you, darling, and she got desperate. They are my fault, really, those scars, every one of them." He could see growing in her eyes that soft amused speculative look which always led to the same thing.

Only two days passed before the next time-bomb went off. When they got up Julia said, "We really ought to change the mattress. We both fall into a kind of hole in the middle."

"I hadn't noticed."

"Lots of people change the mattress every week."

"Yes, Josephine always did."

They stripped the bed and began to roll the mattress. Lying on the springs was a letter addressed to Julia. Carter saw it first and tried to push it out of sight, but Julia saw him.

"What's that?"

"Josephine, of course. There'll soon be too many letters for one volume. We shall have to get them properly edited at Yale like George Eliot's."

"Darling, this is addressed to me. What were you planning to do with it?"

"Destroy it in secret."

"I thought we were going to have no secrets."

"I had counted without Josephine."

For the first time she hesitated before opening the letter. "It's certainly a bit bizarre to put a letter here. Do you think it got there accidentally?"

"Rather difficult, I should think."

She read the letter and then gave it to him. She said with relief, "Oh, she explains why. It's quite natural, really." He read:

Dear Julia, how I hope you are basking in a really Greek sun. Don't tell Philip (oh, but of course you wouldn't have secrets yet), but I never really cared for the south of France. Always that mistral, drying the skin. I'm glad to think you are not suffering there. We always planned to go to Greece when we could afford it, so I know Philip will be happy. I came in today to find a sketch and then remembered that the mattress hadn't been turned for at least a fortnight. We were rather distracted, you know, the last weeks we were together. Anyway, I couldn't bear the thought of your coming back from the lotus islands and finding bumps in your bed the first night, so I've turned it for you. I'd advise you to turn it every week: otherwise a hole always develops in the middle. By the way, I've put up the winter curtains and sent the summer ones to the cleaners at 153 Brompton Road.
Love, Josephine

"If you remember, she wrote to me that Napoule had been heavenly," he said. "The Yale editor will have to put in a cross-reference."

"You *are* a bit cold-blooded," Julia said. "Darling, she's only trying to be helpful. After all, I never knew about the curtains—or the mattress."

"I suppose you are going to write a long cosy letter in reply, full of household chat."

"She's been waiting weeks for an answer. This is an *ancient* letter."

"And I wonder how many more ancient letters there are waiting to pop out. By God, I'm going to search the flat through and through. From attic to basement."

"We don't have either."

"You know very well what I mean."

"I only know you are getting fussed in an exaggerated way. You really behave as though you are frightened of Josephine."

"Oh, hell!"

Julia left the room abruptly and he tried to work. Later that day a squib went off—nothing serious, but it didn't help his mood. He wanted to find the dialing number for overseas telegrams and he discovered inserted in volume one of the directory a complete list in alphabetical order, typed on Josephine's machine on which "o" was always blurred, a complete list of the numbers he most often required. John Hughes, his oldest friend, came after Harrods; and there were the nearest taxi rank, the chemist's, the butcher's, the bank, the dry-cleaner's, the green-grocer's, the fishmonger's, his publisher and agent, Elizabeth Arden's, and the local hairdresser's, marked in brackets ("For J. please note, quite reliable and very inexpensive")—it was the first time he noticed they had the same initials.

Julia who saw him discover the list said, "The angel-woman. We'll pin it up over the telephone. It's really terribly complete."

"After the crack in her last letter I'd have expected her to include Cartier's."

"Darling, it wasn't a crack. It was a bare statement of fact. If I hadn't had a little money, we would have gone to the south of France too."

"I suppose you think I married you to get to Greece."

"Don't be an owl. You don't see Josephine clearly, that's all. You twist every kindness she does."

"Kindness?"

"I expect it's the sense of guilt."

After that he really began a search. He looked in cig-arette-boxes, drawers, filing cabinets, he went through all the pockets of the suits he had left behind, he opened the back of the television cabinet, he lifted the lid of the lavatory cistern, and even changed the roll of toilet paper (it was quicker than unwinding the whole thing). Julia came to look at him, as he worked in the lavatory, without her usual sympathy. He tried the pelmets (who knew what they mightn't discover when next the curtains were sent for cleaning?); he took their dirty clothes out of the basket in case something had been overlooked at the bottom. He went on hands and knees through the kitchen to look under the gas stove, and once when he found a piece of paper wrapped around a pipe, he exclaimed in a kind of triumph, but it was nothing at all—a plumber's relic. The afternoon post rattled through the letter-box and Julia called to him from the hall—"Oh good, you never told me you took in the French *Vogue*."

"I don't."

"Sorry, there's a kind of Christmas card in another envelope. A subscription's been taken out for us by Miss Josephine Heckstall-Jones. I do call that sweet of her."

"She's sold a series of drawings to them. I won't look at it."

"Darling, you are being childish. Do you expect her to stop reading your books?"

"I only want to be left alone with you. Just for a few weeks. It's not so much to ask."

"You're a bit of an egoist, darling."

He felt quiet and tired that evening, but a little relieved in mind. His search had been very thorough. In the middle of dinner he had remembered the wedding presents, still crated for lack of room, and insisted on making sure between the courses that they were still nailed down—he knew Josephine would never have used a screwdriver for fear of injuring her fingers, and she was terrified of hammers. The peace of a solitary evening at last descended on them: the delicious calm which they knew either of them could alter at any moment with a touch of the hand. Lovers cannot postpone as married people can. "I am grown peaceful as old age tonight," he quoted to her.

"Who wrote that?"

"Browning."

"I don't know Browning. Read me some."

He loved to read Browning aloud—he had a good voice for poetry; it was his small harmless narcissism. "Would you really like it?"

"Yes."

"I used to read to Josephine," he warned her.

"What do I care? We can't help doing *some* of the same things, can we, darling?"

"There is something I never read to Josephine. Even though I was in love with her, it wasn't suitable. We weren't—permanent." He began:

"How well I know what I mean to do
When the long dark autumn evenings come. . . ."

He was deeply moved by his own reading. He had never loved Julia so much as at this moment. Here was home— nothing else had been other than a caravan.

". . . I will speak now,
    No longer watch you as you sit
Reading by firelight, that great brow
    And the spirit-small hand propping it,
    Mutely, my heart knows how—"

He rather wished that Julia had really been reading, but then of course she wouldn't have been listening to him with such adorable attention.

"If you join two lives, there is oft a scar.
    They are one and one, with a shadowy third;
One near one is too far."

He turned the page and there lay a sheet of paper (he would have discovered it at once, before reading, if she had put it in an envelope) with the black neat hand-writing.

Dearest Philip, only to say good night to you between the pages of your favourite book—and mine. We are so lucky to have ended in the way we have. With memories in common we shall forever be a little in touch.   Love, Josephine

He flung the book and the paper on the floor. He said, "The bitch. The bloody bitch."

"I won't have you talk of her like that," Julia said with surprising strength. She picked up the paper and read it. "What's wrong with that?" she demanded. "Do you hate memories? What's going to happen to our memories?"

"But don't you see the trick she's playing? Don't you understand? Are you an idiot, Julia?"

That night they lay in bed on opposite sides, not even touching with their feet. It was the first night since they had come home that they had not made love. Neither slept much. In the morning Carter found a letter in the most obvious place of all, which he had somehow neglected: between the leaves of the unused single-lined foolscap on which he always wrote his stories. It began, "Darling, I'm sure you won't mind my using the old old term. . . ."

Cheap in August

I

It was cheap in August: the essential sun, the coral reefs, the bamboo bar and the calypsos—they were all of them at cut prices, like the slightly soiled slips in a bargain sale. Groups arrived periodically from Philadelphia in the manner of school-treats and departed with less *bruit*, after an exact exhausting week, when the picnic was over. Perhaps for twenty-four hours the swimming pool and the bar were almost deserted, and then another school-treat would arrive, this time from St. Louis. Everyone knew everyone else; they had bussed together to an airport, they had flown together, together they had faced an alien customs; they would separate during the day and greet each other noisily and happily after dark, exchanging impressions of "shooting the rapids," the botanic gardens, the Spanish fort. "We are doing that tomorrow."

Mary Watson wrote to her husband in Europe, "I had to get away for a bit and it's so cheap in August." They

had been married ten years and they had only been separated three times. He wrote to her every day and the
letters arrived twice a week in little bundles. She arranged them like newspapers by the date and read them
in the correct order. They were tender and precise; what
with his research, with preparing lectures and writing
letters he had little time to *see* Europe—he insisted on
calling it "your Europe" as though to assure her that he
had not forgotten the sacrifice which she must have
made by marrying an American professor from New
England, but sometimes little criticisms of "her Europe"
escaped him—the food was too rich, cigarettes too expensive, wine too often served, and milk very difficult to
obtain at lunchtime—which might indicate that, after
all, she ought not to exaggerate her sacrifice. Perhaps it
would have been a good thing if James Thomson, who
was his special study at the moment, had written *The
Seasons* in America—an American autumn, she had to
admit, was more beautiful than an English one.

Mary Watson wrote to him every other day, but sometimes a postcard only, and she was apt to forget if she
had repeated the postcard. She wrote in the shade of the
bamboo bar, where she could see everyone who passed
on the way to the swimming pool. She wrote truthfully,
"It's so cheap in August; the hotel is not half full, and
the heat and the humidity are very tiring. But, of course,
it's a change." She had no wish to appear extravagant;
the salary, which to her European eyes had seemed
astronomically large for a professor of literature, had
long dwindled to its proper proportions, relative to the
price of steaks and salads—she must justify with a little

enthusiasm the money she was spending in his absence.
So she wrote also about the flowers in the botanic gardens—she had ventured that far on one occasion—and
with less truth of the beneficial changes wrought by the
sun and the lazy life on her friend Margaret who from
"her England" had written and demanded her company:
a Margaret, she admitted frankly to herself, who was
not visible to any eye but the eye of faith. But then
Charlie had complete faith. Even good qualities become
with the erosion of time a reproach. After ten years of
being happily married, she thought, one undervalues
security and tranquillity.

She read Charlie's letters with great attention. She
longed to find in them one ambiguity, one evasion, one
time-gap which he had ill-explained. Even an unusually
strong expression of love would have pleased her, for its
strength might have been there to counterweigh a sense
of guilt. But she couldn't deceive herself that there was
any sense of guilt in Charlie's facile flowing informative
script. She calculated that if he had been one of the
poets he was now so closely studying, he would have
completed already a standard-sized epic during his first
two months in "her Europe," and the letters, after all,
were only a spare-time occupation. They filled up the
vacant hours, and certainly they could have left no room
for any other occupation. "It is ten o'clock at night, it is
raining outside and the temperature is rather cool for
August, not above fifty-six degrees. When I have said
good night to you, dear one, I shall go happily to bed
with the thought of you. I have a long day tomorrow at
the museum and dinner in the evening with the Henry

Wilkinsons who are passing through on their way from Athens—you remember the Henry Wilkinsons, don't you?" (Didn't she just?) She had wondered whether, when Charlie returned, she might perhaps detect some small unfamiliar note in his love-making which would indicate that a stranger had passed that way. Now she disbelieved in the possibility, and anyway the evidence would arrive too late—it was no good to her now that she might be justified later. She wanted her justification immediately, a justification not—alas!—for any act that she had committed but only for an intention, for the intention of betraying Charlie, of having, like so many of her friends, a holiday affair (the idea had come to her immediately the dean's wife had said, "It's so cheap in Jamaica in August").

The trouble was that, after three weeks of calypsos in the humid evening, the rum punches (for which she could no longer disguise from herself a repugnance), the warm martinis, the interminable red snappers, and tomatoes with everything, there had been no affair, not even the hint of one. She had discovered with disappointment the essential morality of a holiday resort in the cheap season; there were no opportunities for infidelity, only for writing postcards—with great brilliant blue skies and seas—to Charlie. Once a woman from St. Louis had taken too obvious pity on her, when she sat alone in the bar writing postcards, and invited her to join their party, which was about to visit the botanic gardens—"We are an awfully jolly bunch," she had said with a big turnip smile. Mary exaggerated her English accent to repel her better and said that she didn't much care for flowers. It had shocked the woman as deeply as if she had said she did not care for television. From the motion of the heads at the other end of the bar, the agitated clinking of the Coca-Cola glasses, she could tell that her words were being repeated from one to another. Afterwards, until the jolly bunch had taken the airport limousine on the way back to St. Louis, she was aware of averted heads. She was English, she had taken a superior attitude to flowers, and as she preferred even warm martinis to Coca-Cola, she was probably in their eyes an alcoholic.

It was a feature common to most of these jolly bunches that they contained no male attachment, and perhaps that was why the attempt to look attractive was completely abandoned. Huge buttocks were exposed in their full horror in tight large-patterned Bermuda shorts. Heads were bound in scarves to cover rollers which were not removed even by lunch-time—they stuck out like small mole-hills. Daily she watched the bums lurch by like hippos on the way to the water. Only in the evening would the women change from the monstrous shorts into monstrous cotton frocks, covered with mauve or scarlet flowers, in order to take dinner on the terrace, where formality was demanded in the book of rules, and the few men who appeared were forced to wear jackets and ties though the thermometer stood at close on eighty degrees after sunset. The market in femininity being such, how could one hope to see any male foragers? Only old and broken husbands were sometimes to be seen towed towards an Issa store advertising free-port prices.

She had been encouraged during the first week by
the sight of three young men with crew-cuts who went
past the bar towards the swimming-pool wearing male
bikinis. They were far too young for her, but in her
present mood she would have welcomed altruistically
the sight of another's romance. Romance is said to be
contagious, and if in the candle-lit evenings the "infor-
mal" coffee-tavern had contained a few young amorous
couples, who could say what men of maturer years
might not eventually arrive to catch the infection? But
her hopes dwindled. The young men came and went
without a glance at the Bermuda shorts or the pinned
hair. Why should they stay? They were certainly more
beautiful than any girl there and they knew it.

By nine o'clock most evenings Mary Watson was on
her way to bed. A few evenings of calypsos, of quaint
false impromptus, and the hideous jangle of rattles had
been enough. Outside the closed windows of the hotel-
annexe the boxes of the air-conditioners made a continu-
ous rumble in the starry palmy night like over-fed hotel
guests. Her room was full of dried air which bore no
more resemblance to fresh air than the dried figs to the
newly picked fruit. When she looked in the glass to
brush her hair she often regretted her lack of charity to
the jolly bunch from St. Louis. It was true she did not
wear Bermuda shorts nor coil her hair in rollers, but her
hair was streaky none the less with heat and the mirror
reflected more plainly than it seemed to do at home her
thirty-nine years. If she had not paid an advance for a
four weeks *pension* on her individual round-trip tour,
with tickets exchangeable for a variety of excursions,

she would have turned tail and returned to the campus. Next year, she thought, when I am forty, I must feel grateful that I have preserved the love of a good man.

She was a woman given to self-analysis, and perhaps because it is a great deal easier to direct questions to a particular face rather than to a void (one has the right to expect some kind of a response even from eyes one sees many times a day in a compact), she posed the questions to herself with a belligerent direct stare into the looking-glass. She was an honest woman, and for that reason the questions were all the cruder. She would say to herself: I have slept with no one other than Charlie (she wouldn't admit as sexual experiences the small exciting halfway points that she reached before marriage); why am I now seeking to find a strange body, which will probably give me less pleasure than the body I already know? It had been more than a month before Charlie brought her real pleasure. Pleasure, she learnt, grew with habit, so that if it were not really pleasure that she looked for, what was it? The answer could be only the unfamiliar. She had friends, even on the respectable campus, who had admitted to her, in the frank admirable American way, their adventures. These had usually been in Europe—a momentary marital absence had given the opportunity for a momentary excitement, and then with what a sigh of relief they had found themselves safely at home. All the same they felt afterwards that they had enlarged their experience; they understood something that their husbands did not really understand—the real character of a Frenchman, an Italian, even—there were such cases—of an Englishman.

Mary Watson was painfully aware, as an English-woman, that her experience was confined to one American. They all, on the campus, believed her to be European, but all she knew was confined to one man and he was a citizen of Boston who had no curiosity for the great Western regions. In a sense she was more American by choice than he was by birth. Perhaps she was less European even than the wife of the Professor of Romance Languages, who had confided to her that once —overwhelmingly—in Antibes . . . it had happened only once because the sabbatical year was over . . . her husband was up in Paris checking manuscripts before they flew home. . . .

Had she herself, Mary Watson sometimes wondered, been just such a European adventure which Charlie mistakenly had domesticated? (She couldn't pretend to be a tigress in a cage, but they kept smaller creatures in cages, white mice, love-birds). And to be fair Charlie too was her adventure, her American adventure, the kind of man whom at twenty-seven she had not before encountered in frowsy London. Henry James had described the type, and at that moment in her history she had been reading a great deal of Henry James: "A man of intellect whose body was not much to him and its senses and appetites not importunate." All the same, for a while she had made the appetites importunate.

That was her private conquest of the American continent, and when the Professor's wife had spoken of the dancer of Antibes (no, that was a Roman inscription— the man had been a *marchand de vin*) she had thought: the lover I know and admire is American and I am

proud of it. But afterwards came the thought: American
or New England? Yet to know a country must one know
every region sexually?

It was absurd at thirty-nine not to be content. She
had her man. The book on James Thomson would be
published by the University Press, and Charlie had the
intention afterwards of making a revolutionary break
from the romantic poetry of the eighteenth century into
a study of the American image in European literature—
it was to be called *The Double Reflection;* the effect
of Fenimore Cooper on the European scene: the image
of America presented by Mrs. Trollope—the details
were not yet worked out. The study might possibly end
with the first arrival of Dylan Thomas on the shores of
America—at the Cunard quay or at Idlewild? That was
a point for later research. She examined herself again
closely in the glass—the new decade of the forties
stared frankly back at her—an Englander who had become a New Englander. After all, she hadn't travelled
very far—Kent to Connecticut. This was not just the
physical restlessness of middle age, she argued; it was
the universal desire to see a little bit further, before one
surrendered to old age and the blank certitude of death.

II

Next day she picked up her courage and went as far as
the swimming-pool. A strong wind blew and whipped
up the waves in the almost land-girt harbour—the hur-
ricane season would soon be here. All the world creaked
around her: the wooden struts of the shabby harbour,

the jalousies of the small hopeless houses which looked as though they had been knocked together from a make-it-yourself kit, the branches of the palms—a long, weary, worn-out creaking. Even the water of the swimming pool imitated in miniature the waves of the harbour.

She was glad that she was alone in the swimming-pool, at least for all practical purposes alone, for the old man splashing water over himself, like an elephant, in the shallow end hardly counted. He was a solitary elephant and not one of the hippo band. They would have called her with merry cries to join them—and it's difficult to be stand-offish in a swimming pool, which is common to all as a table is not. They might even in their resentment have ducked her—pretending like school children that it was all a merry game; there was nothing she put beyond those thick thighs, whether they were encased in bikinis or Bermuda shorts. As she floated in the pool her ears were alert for their approach. At the first sound she would get well away from the water, but today they were probably making an excursion to Tower Isle on the other side of the island, or had they done that yesterday? Only the old man watched her, pouring water over his head to keep away sun-stroke. She was safely alone, which was the next best thing to the adventure she had come here to find. All the same, as she sat on the rim of the pool and let the sun and wind dry her, she realized the extent of her solitude. She had spoken to no one but black waiters and Syrian receptionists for more than two weeks. Soon, she thought, I shall even begin to miss Charlie—it would be an ignoble finish to what she had intended to be an adventure.

A voice from the water said to her, "My name's Hick-slaughter—Henry Hickslaughter." She couldn't have sworn to the name in court, but that was how it had sounded at the time, and he never repeated it. She looked down at a polished mahogany crown surrounded by white hair; perhaps he resembled Neptune more than an elephant. Neptune was always outsize, and, as he had pulled himself a little out of the water to speak, she could see the rolls of fat folding over the blue bathing-slip, with tough hair lying like weeds along the ditches. She replied with amusement, "My name is Watson. Mary Watson."

"You're English?"

"My husband's American," she said in extenuation.

"I haven't seen him around, have I?"

"He's in England," she said with a small sigh, for the geographical and national situation seemed too compli-cated for casual explanation.

"You like it here?" he asked and lifting a hand-cup of water he distributed it over his bald head.

"So-so."

"Got the time on you?"

She looked in her bag and told him, "Eleven-fifteen."

"I've had my half hour," he said and trod heavily away towards the ladder at the shallow end.

An hour later, staring at her lukewarm martini with its great green unappetizing olive, she saw him looming down at her from the other end of the bamboo bar. He

wore an ordinary shirt open at the neck and a brown
leather belt; his type of shoes in her childhood had been
known as co-respondent, but one seldom saw them
today. She wondered what Charlie would think of her
pick-up; unquestionably she had landed him, rather as
an angler struggling with a heavy catch finds that he
has hooked nothing better than an old boot. She was no
angler; she didn't know whether a boot would put an
ordinary hook out of action altogether, but she knew
that *her* hook could be irremediably damaged. No one
would approach her if she were in his company. She
drained the martini in one gulp and even attacked the
olive so as to have no excuse to linger in the bar.

"Would you do me the honour," Mr. Hickslaughter
asked, "of having a drink with me?" His manner was
completely changed; on dry land he seemed unsure of
himself and spoke with an old-fashioned propriety.

"I'm afraid I've only just finished one. I have to be
off." Inside the gross form she thought she saw a tousled
child with disappointed eyes. "I'm having lunch early
today." She got up and added rather stupidly, for the
bar was quite empty, "You can have my table."

"I don't need a drink that much," he said solemnly. "I
was just after company." She knew that he was watching her as she moved to the adjoining coffee tavern, and
she thought with guilt, At least I've got the old boot off
the hook. She refused the shrimp cocktail with tomato
ketchup and fell back as was usual with her on a grape-
fruit, with grilled trout to follow. "Please no tomato with
the trout," she implored, but the black waiter obviously
didn't understand her. While she waited she began with

amusement to picture a scene between Charlie and Mr. Hickslaughter, who happened for the purpose of her story to be crossing the campus. "This is Henry Hickslaughter, Charlie. We used to go bathing together when I was in Jamaica." Charlie, who always wore English clothes, was very tall, very thin, very concave. It was a satisfaction to know that he would never lose his figure —his nerves would see to that, and his extreme sensibility. He hated anything gross; there was no grossness in *The Seasons,* not even in the lines on spring.

She heard slow footsteps coming up behind her and nearly panicked. "May I share your table?" Mr. Hickslaughter asked. He had recovered his terrestrial politeness, but only so far as speech was concerned, for he sat firmly down without waiting for her reply. The chair was too small for him; his thighs overlapped like a double mattress on a single bed. He began to study the menu.

"They copy American food; it's worse than the reality," Mary Watson said.

"You don't like American food?"

"Tomatoes even with the trout!"

"Tomatoes? Oh, you mean tomatoes," he said, correcting her accent. "I'm fond of tomatoes myself."

"And fresh pineapple in the salad."

"There's a lot of vitamins in fresh pineapple." Almost as if he wished to emphasize their disagreement, he ordered shrimp cocktail, grilled trout, and a sweet salad. Of course, when her trout arrived, the tomatoes were there. "You can have mine if you want to,"she said, and he accepted with pleasure. "You are very kind. You are really very kind." He held out his plate like Oliver Twist.

She began to feel oddly at ease with the old man. She would have been less at ease, she was certain, with a possible adventure: she would have been wondering about her effect on him, while now she could be sure that she gave him pleasure—with the tomatoes. He was perhaps less the old anonymous boot than an old shoe comfortable to wear. And curiously enough, in spite of his first approach and in spite of his correcting her over the pronunciation of tomatoes, it was not really an old American shoe of which she was reminded. Charlie wore English clothes over his English figure, he studied English eighteenth-century literature, his book would be published in England by the Cambridge University Press who would buy sheets, but she had the impression that he was far more fashioned as an American shoe than Hickslaughter. Even Charlie, whose manners were perfect, if they had met for the first time today at the swimming pool, would have interrogated her more closely. Interrogation had always seemed to her a principal part of American social life—an inheritance perhaps from the Indian smoke-fires. "Where are you from? Do you know the So-and-so's? Have you been to the botanic gardens?" It came over her that Mr. Hickslaughter, if that were really his name, was perhaps an American reject—not necessarily more flawed than the pottery rejects of famous firms you find in bargain-basements.

She found herself questioning *him*, with circumlocutions, while he savoured the tomatoes. "I was born in London. I couldn't have been born more than four hundred miles from there without drowning, could I? But you belong to a continent thousands of miles wide and long. Where were you born?" (She remembered a character in a Western movie directed by John Ford who asked, "Where do you hail from, stranger?" The question was more frankly put than hers.)

He said, "St. Louis."

"Oh, then there are lots of your people here—you are not alone." She felt a slight disapppointment that he might belong to the jolly bunch.

"I'm alone," he said. "Room sixty-three." It was in her own corridor on the third floor of the annexe. He spoke firmly, as though he were imparting information for future use. "Five doors down from you."

"Oh."

"I saw you come out your first day."

"I never noticed you."

"I keep to myself unless I see someone I like."

"Didn't you see anyone you liked from St. Louis?"

"I'm not all that fond of St. Louis, and St. Louis can do without me. I'm not a favourite son."

"Do you come here often"

"In August. It's cheap in August." He kept on surprising her. First there was his lack of local patriotism, and now his frankness about money or rather about the lack of it, a frankness that could almost be classed as an un-American activity.

"Yes."

"I have to go where it's reasonable," he said, as though he were exposing his bad hand to a partner at gin.

"You've retired?"

"Well—I've been retired." He added, "You ought to take salad. . . . It's good for you."

"I feel quite well without it."

"You could do with more weight." He added appraisingly, "A couple of pounds." She was tempted to tell him that he could do with less. They had both seen each other exposed.

"Were you in business?" She was being driven to interrogate. He hadn't asked her a personal question since his first at the pool.

"In a way," he said. She had a sense that he was supremely uninterested in his own doings; she was certainly discovering an America which she had not known existed.

She said, "Well, if you'll excuse me . . ."

"Aren't you taking any dessert?"

"No, I'm a light luncher."

"It's all included in the price. You ought to eat some fruit." He was looking at her under his white eyebrows with an air of disappointment which touched her.

"I don't care much for fruit and I want a nap. I always have a nap in the afternoon."

Perhaps, after all, she thought, as she moved away through the formal dining-room, he is disappointed only because I'm not taking full advantage of the cheap rate.

She passed his room going to her own: the door was open and a big white-haired mammy was making the bed. The room was exactly like her own—the same pair of double beds, the same wardrobe, the same dressing-table in the same position, the same heavy breathing of the air-conditioner. In her own room she looked in vain for the Thermos of iced water; then she rang the bell and waited for several minutes. You couldn't expect good service in August. She went down the passage; Mr. Hickslaughter's door was still open, and she went in to find the maid. The door of the bathroom was open too, and a wet cloth lay on the tiles.

How bare the bedroom was. At least she had taken the trouble to add a few flowers, a photograph, and half a dozen books on a bedside table, which gave her room a lived-in air. Beside his bed there was only a digest magazine lying open and face down; she turned it over to see what he was reading—as she might have expected, it was something to do with calories and proteins. He had begun writing a letter at his dressing-table and with the simple unscrupulousness of an intellectual she began to read it with her ears cocked for any sound in the passage.

"Dear Joe," she read, "the draft was two weeks late last month and I was in real difficulties. I had to borrow from a Syrian who runs a tourist junk-shop in Curaçao and pay him interest. You owe me a hundred dollars for the interest. It's your own fault. Mom never gave us lessons on how to live on an empty stomach. Please add it to the next draft and be sure to do that, you wouldn't want me coming back to collect. I'll be here till the end of August. It's cheap in August, and a man gets tired of nothing but Dutch, Dutch, Dutch. Give my love to Sis."

The letter broke off unfinished. Anyway, she would have had no opportunity to read more because someone was approaching down the passage. She went to the door in time to see Mr. Hickslaughter on the threshold. He said, "You looking for me?"

"I was looking for the maid. She was in here a minute ago."

"Come in and sit down."

He looked through the bathroom door and then at the room in general. Perhaps it was only an uneasy conscience which made her think that his eyes strayed a moment to the unfinished letter.

"She's forgotten my iced water."

"You can have mine if it's filled." He shook his Thermos and handed it to her.

"Thanks a lot."

"When you've had your sleep—" he began and looked away from her. Was he looking at the letter?

"Yes?"

"We might have a drink."

She was, in a sense, trapped. She said, "Yes."

"Give me a ring when you wake up."

"Yes." She said nervously, "have a good sleep yourself."

"Oh, I don't sleep." He didn't wait for her to leave the room before turning away, swinging that great elephantine backside of his towards her. She had walked into a trap baited with a flask of iced water, and in her room she drank the water gingerly as though it might have a flavour different from hers.

III

She found it difficult to sleep: the old fat man had become an individual now that she had read his letter. She couldn't help comparing his style with Charlie's. "When I have said good night to you, my dear one, I shall go happily to bed with the thought of you." In Mr. Hickslaughter's there was an ambiguity, a hint of menace. Was it possible that the old man could be dangerous?

At half past five she rang up room 63. It was not the kind of adventure she had planned, but it was an adventure none the less. "I'm awake," she said.

"You coming for a drink?" he asked.

"I'll meet you in the bar."

"Not the bar," he said. "Not at the prices they charge for bourbon. I've got all we need here."

She felt as though she were being brought back to the scene of a crime, and she needed a little courage to knock on the door.

He had everything prepared: a bottle of Old Walker, a bucket of ice, two bottles of soda. Like books, drinks can make a room inhabited. She saw him as a man fighting in his own fashion against the sense of solitude.

"Siddown," he said, "make yourself comfortable," like a character in a movie. He began to pour out two highballs.

She said, "I've got an awful sense of guilt. I did come in here for iced water, but I was curious too. I read your letter."

"I knew someone had touched it," he said.

"I'm sorry."

"Who cares? It was only to my brother."

"I had no business . . ."

"Look," he said, "if I came into your room and found a letter open I'd read it, wouldn't I? Only your letter would be more interesting."

"Why?"

"I don't write love letters. Never did and I'm too old now." He sat down on a bed—she had the only easy chair. His belly hung in heavy folds under his sports shirt, and his fly was a little open. Why was it always fat men who left them unbuttoned? He said, "This is good bourbon," taking a drain of it. "What does your husband do?" he asked—it was his first personal question since the pool, and it took her by surprise.

"He writes about literature. Eighteenth-century poetry," she added, rather inanely under the circumstances.

"Oh."

"What did you do? I mean when you worked."

"This and that."

"And now?"

"I watch what goes on. Sometimes I talk to someone like you. Well, no, I don't suppose I've ever talked to anyone like you before." It might have seemed a compliment if he had not added, "A professor's wife."

"And you read the *Digest?*"

"Ye-eh. They make books too long—I haven't the patience. Eighteenth-century poetry. So they wrote poetry back in those days, did they?"

She said, "Yes," not sure whether or not he was mocking her.

"There was a poem I liked at school. The only one that ever stuck in my head. By Longfellow, I think. You ever read Longfellow?"

"Not really. They don't read him much in school any longer."

"Something about Spanish sailors with bearded lips and the something and mystery of the ships and the something of the sea. It hasn't stuck all that well, after all, but I suppose I learned that sixty years ago and even more. Those were the days."

"The nineteen-hundreds?"

"No, no. I meant pirates—Kidd and Bluebeard and those fellows. This was their stamping ground, wasn't it? The Caribbean. It makes you kind of sick to see those women going around in their shorts here." His tongue had been tingled into activity by the bourbon.

It occurred to her that she had never really been curious about another human being; she had been in love with Charlie, but he hadn't aroused her curiosity except sexually, and she had satisfied that only too quickly. She asked him, "Do you love your sister?"

"Yes, of course, why? How do you know I've got a sister?"

"And Joe?"

"You certainly read my letter. Oh, he's O.K."

"O.K.?"

"Well you know how it is with brothers. I'm the oldest in my family. There was one that died. My sister's twenty years younger than I am. Joe's got the means. He looks after her."

"You haven't got the means?"

"I had the means. I wasn't good at managing them, though. We aren't here to talk about myself."

"I'm curious. That's why I read your letter."

"You? Curious about me?"

"It could be, couldn't it?"

She had confused him, and now that she had the upper hand, she felt that she was out of the trap; she was free, she could come and go as she pleased, and if she chose to stay a little longer, it was her own choice.

"Have another bourbon?" he said. "But you're English. Maybe you'd prefer Scotch?"

"Better not mix."

"No." He poured her another glass. He said, "I was wondering—sometimes I want to get away from this joint for a little. What about having dinner down the road?"

"It would be stupid," she said. "We've both paid our *pension* here, haven't we? And it would be the same dinner in the end. Red snapper. Tomatoes."

"I don't know what you have against tomatoes," but he did not deny the good sense of her economic reasoning: he was the first unsuccessful American she had ever had a drink with. One must have seen them in the street . . . But even the young men who came to the house were not yet unsuccessful. The Professor of Romance Languages had perhaps hoped to be head of a university—success is relative, but it remains success.

He poured out another glass. She said, "I'm drinking all your bourbon."

"It's in a good cause."

She was a little drunk by now and things—which only *seemed* relevant—came to her mind. She said, "That thing of Longfellow's. It went on—something about 'the thoughts of youth are long long thoughts.' I must have read it somewhere. That was the refrain, wasn't it?"

"Maybe. I don't remember."

"Did you want to be a pirate when you were a boy?"

He gave an almost happy grin. He said, "I succeeded. That's what Joe called me once—'pirate.'"

"But you haven't any buried treasure?"

He said, "He knows me well enough not to send me a hundred dollars. But if he feels scared enough that I'll come back—he might send fifty. And the interest was only twenty-five. He's not mean, but he's stupid."

"How?"

"He ought to know I wouldn't go back. I wouldn't do one thing to hurt Sis."

"Would it be any good if I asked you to have dinner with me?"

"No. It wouldn't be right." In some ways he was obviously very conservative. "It's as you said—you don't want to go throwing money about." When the bottle of Old Walker was half empty, he said, "You'd better have some food even if it is red snapper and tomatoes."

"Is your name really Hickslaughter?"

"Something like that."

They went downstairs, following rather carefully in each other's footsteps like ducks. In the formal restaurant open to all the heat of the evening, the men sat and sweated in their jackets and ties. They passed, the two of them, through the bamboo bar into the coffee tavern, which was lit by candles that increased the heat. Two young men with crew-cuts sat at the next table—they weren't the same young men she had seen before, but they came out of the same series. One of them said, "I'm not denying that he has a certain style, but even if you *adore* Tennessee Williams . . ."

"Why did he call you a pirate?"

"It was just one of those things."

When it came to the decision there seemed nothing to choose except red snapper and tomatoes, and again she offered him her tomatoes; perhaps he had grown to expect it, and already she was chained by custom. He was an old man, he had made no pass which she could reasonably reject—how could a man of his age make a pass to a woman of hers?—and yet all the same she had a sense that she had landed on a conveyor belt. . . . The future was not in her hands, and she was a little scared. She would have been more frightened if it had not been for her unusual consumption of bourbon.

"It was good bourbon," she commented for something to say, and immediately regretted it. It gave him an opening.

"We'll take another glass before bed."

"I think I've drunk enough."

"A good bourbon won't hurt you. You'll sleep well."

"I always sleep well." It was a lie—the kind of un-important lie one tells a husband or a lover in order to keep some privacy. The young man who had been talking about Tennessee Williams rose from his table. He was very tall and thin and he wore a skin-tight black sweater; his small elegant buttocks were outlined in skin-tight trousers. It was easy to imagine him a degree more naked. Would he have looked at her, she wondered, with any interest if she had not been sitting there in the company of a fat old man so horribly clothed? It was unlikely; his body was not designed for a woman's caress.

"I don't."

"You don't what?"

"I don't sleep well." The unexpected self-disclosure after all his reticences came as a shock. It was as though he had put out one of his square brick-like hands and pulled her to him. He had been aloof, he had evaded her personal questions, he had lured her into a sense of security, but now every time she opened her mouth she seemed doomed to commit an error, to invite him nearer. Even her harmless remark about the bourbon . . . She said stupidly, "Perhaps it's the change of climate."

"What change of climate?"

"Between here and . . . and . . ."

"Curaçao? I guess there's no great difference. I don't sleep there either."

"I've got some very good pills . . ." she said rashly.

"I thought you said you slept well."

"Oh, there are always times. It's sometimes just a question of digestion."

"Yes, digestion. You're right there. A bourbon will be good for that. If you've finished dinner . . ."

She looked across the coffee tavern to the bamboo bar, where the young man stood *déhanché*, holding a glass of crème de menthe between his face and his companion's like an exotically coloured monocle.

Mr. Hickslaughter said in a shocked voice, "You don't care for that type, do you?"

"They're often good conversationalists."

"Oh, conversation . . . If that's what you want." It was as though she had expressed an un-American liking for snails or frogs' legs.

"Shall we have our bourbon in the bar? It's a little cooler tonight."

"And listen to their chatter? No, we'll go upstairs."

He swung back again in the direction of old-fashioned courtesy and came behind her to pull her chair—even Charlie was not so polite, but was it politeness or the determination to block her way of escape to the bar?

They entered the lift together. The black attendant had a radio turned on, and from the small brown box came the voice of a preacher talking about the Blood of the Lamb. Perhaps it was a Sunday, and that would explain the temporary void around them—between one jolly bunch and another. They stepped out into the empty corridor like undesirables marooned. The boy followed them out and sat down upon a chair beside the elevator to wait for another signal, while the voice continued to talk about the Blood of the Lamb. What was she afraid of? Mr. Hickslaughter began to unlock his door. He was much older than her father would have been if he had been still alive; he could be her grandfather—the excuse, "What will the boy think?" was inadmissible—it was even shocking, for his manner had never ceased to be correct. He might be old, but what right had she to think of him as "dirty"?

"Damn the hotel-key," he said. "It won't open."

She turned the handle for him. "The door wasn't locked."

"I can sure do with a bourbon after those nancies. . . ."

But now she had her excuse ready on the lips. "I've had one too many already, I'm afraid. I've got to sleep it off." She put her hand on his arm. "Thank you so much, . . . It was a lovely evening." She was aware how insulting her English accent sounded as she walked quickly down the corridor leaving it behind her like a mocking presence, mocking all the things she liked best in him: his ambiguous character, his memory of Longfellow, his having to make ends meet.

She looked back when she reached her room: he was standing in the passage as though he couldn't make up his mind to go in. She was reminded of an old man whom she had passed one day on the campus leaning on his broom among the unswept autumn leaves.

IV

In her room she picked up a book and tried to read. It was Thomson's *Seasons*. She had carried it with her, so that she could understand any references to his work that Charlie might make in a letter. This was the first time she had opened it, and she was not held:

> And now the mounting Sun dispels the Fog:
> The rigid Hoar-Frost melts before his Beam;
> And hung on every Spray, on every Blade
> Of Grass, the myriad Dew-Drops twinkle round.

If she could be so cowardly, she thought, with a harmless old man like that, how could she have faced the real decisiveness of an adventure? One was not, at her age, "swept off the feet." Charlie had been proved just as sadly right to trust her as she was right to trust Charlie. Now with the difference in time he would be leaving the Museum, or rather, if this were a Sunday as the Blood of the Lamb seemed to indicate, he would probably have just quit writing in his hotel room. After a successful day's work he always resembled an advertisement for a new shaving-cream: a kind of glow . . . She found it irritating, like living with a halo. Even his voice had a different timbre and he would call her "old girl" and pat her bottom patronizingly. She preferred him when he was touchy with failure: only temporary failure, of course, the failure of an idea which hadn't worked out, the touchiness of a child's disappointment at a party which has not come up to his expectations, not the failure of the old man—the rusted framework of a ship transfixed once and for all upon the rock where it had struck.

She felt ignoble. What earthly risk could the old man represent to justify refusing him half an hour's companionship? He could no more assault her than the boat could detach itself from the rock and steam out to sea for the Fortunate Islands. She pictured him sitting alone with his half-empty bottle of bourbon seeking unconsciousness. Or was he perhaps finishing the crude blackmailing letter to his brother? What a story she would make of it one day, she thought with self-disgust as she took off her dress, her evening with a blackmailer and "pirate."

There was one thing she could do for him: she could give him her bottle of pills. She put on her dressing-gown and retrod the corridor, room by room, until she arrived at 63. His voice told her to come in. She opened the door and in the light of the bedside lamp saw him sitting on the edge of the bed wearing a crumpled pair of cotton pyjamas with broad mauve stripes. She began, "I've brought you . . ." and then she saw to her amazement that he had been crying. His eyes were red and the evening darkness of his cheeks sparkled with points like dew. She had only once before seen a man cry— Charlie, when the University Press had decided against his first volume of literary essays.

"I thought you were the maid," he said. "I rang for her."

"What did you want?"

"I thought she might take a glass of bourbon," he said.

"Did you want so much . . . I'll take a glass." The bottle was still on the dressing-table, where they had left it and the two glasses—she identified hers by the smear of lipstick. "Here you are," she said, "drink it up. It will make you sleep."

He said, "I'm not an alcoholic."

"Of course you aren't."

She sat on the bed beside him and took his left hand in hers. It was cracked and dry, and she wanted to clean back the cuticle until she remembered that was something she did for Charlie.

"I wanted company," he said.

"I'm here."

"You better turn off the bell-light or the maid will come."

"She'll never know what she missed in the way of Old Walker."

When she returned from the door he was lying back against the pillows in an odd twisted position, and she thought again of the ship broken-backed upon the rocks. She tried to pick up his feet to lay them on the bed, but they were like heavy stones at the bottom of a quarry.

"Lie down," she said "You'll never be sleepy that way. What do you do for company in Curaçao?"

"I manage," he said.

"You've finished the bourbon. Let me put out the lights."

"It's no good pretending to you," he said.

"Pretending?"

"I'm afraid of the dark."

She thought, I'll smile later when I think of who it was I feared. She said, "Do the old pirates you fought come back to haunt you?"

"I've done some bad things," he said, "in my time."

"Haven't we all?"

"Nothing extraditable," he explained as though that were an extenuation.

"If you take one of my pills . . ."

"You won't go—not yet?"

"No, no. I'll stay till you're sleepy."

"I've been wanting to talk to you for days."

"I'm glad you did."

"Would you believe it—I didn't have the nerve." If she had shut her eyes it might have been a very young man speaking. "I don't know your sort."

"Don't you have my sort in Curaçao?"

"No."

"You haven't taken the pill yet."

"I'm afraid of not waking up."

"Have you so much to do tomorrow?"

"I mean ever." He put out his hand and touched her knee, searchingly, without sensuality, as if he needed support from the bone. "I'll tell you what's wrong. You're a stranger, so I can tell you. I'm afraid of dying, with nobody around, in the dark."

"Are you ill?"

"I wouldn't know. I don't see doctors. I don't like doctors."

"But why should you think . . . ?"

"I'm over seventy. The Bible age. It could happen any day now."

"You'll live to a hundred," she said with an odd conviction.

"Then I'll have to live with fear a hell of a long time."

"Was that why you were crying?"

"No. I thought you were going to stay awhile, and then suddenly you went. I guess I was disappointed."

"Are you never alone in Curaçao?"

"I pay not to be alone."

"As you'd have paid the maid?"

"Ye-eh. Sort of."

It was as though she were discovering for the first time the interior of the enormous continent on which she had elected to live. America had been Charlie, it had been New England; through books and movies she had been aware of the wonders of nature like some great Cinerama film with Lowell Thomas cheapening the Painted Desert and the Grand Canyon with his clichés. There had been no mystery anywhere from Miami to Niagara Falls, from Cape Cod to the Pacific Palisades; tomatoes were served on every plate and Coca-Cola in every glass. Nobody anywhere admitted failure or fear; they were like "sins hushed up"—worse perhaps than sins, for sins have glamour—they were bad taste. But here stretched on the bed, dressed in striped pyjamas which Brooks Brothers would have disowned, failure and fear talked to her without shame, and in an American accent. It was as though she were living in the remote future, after God knew what catastrophe.

She said, "I wasn't for sale? There was only the Old Walker to tempt *me*."

He raised his antique Neptune head a little way from the pillow and said, "I'm not afraid of death. Not sudden death. Believe me, I've looked for it here and there. It's this certain-sure business, closing in on you, like tax-inspectors. . . ."

She said, "Sleep now."

"I can't."

"Yes, you can."

"If you'd stay with me awhile . . ."

"I'll stay with you. Relax." She lay down on the bed beside him on the outside of the sheet. In a few minutes he was deeply asleep and she turned off the light. He grunted several times and spoke only once, when he said, "You've got me wrong," and after that he became for a little while like a dead man in his immobility and his silence, so that during that period she fell asleep. When she woke she was aware from his breathing that he was awake too. He was lying away from her so that their bodies wouldn't touch. She put out her hand and felt no repulsion at all at his excitement. It was as though she had spent many nights beside him in the one bed, and when he made love to her, silently and abruptly in the darkness, she gave a sigh of satisfaction. There was no guilt; she would be going back in a few days, resigned and tender, to Charlie and Charlie's loving skill, and she wept a little, but not seriously, at the temporary nature of this meeting.

"What's wrong?" he asked.

"Nothing. Nothing. I wish I could stay."

"Stay a little longer. Stay till it's light." That would not be very long. Already they could distinguish the grey masses of the furniture standing around them like Caribbean tombs.

"Oh, yes, I'll stay till it's light. That wasn't what I meant." His body began to slip out of her, and it was as though he were carrying away her unknown child, away in the direction of Curaçao, and she tried to hold him back, the fat old frightened man whom she almost loved.

He said, "I never had this in mind."

"I know. Don't say it. I understand."

"I guess after all we've got a lot in common," he said, and she agreed in order to quieten him. He was fast asleep by the time the light came back, so she got off the bed without waking him and went to her room. She locked the door and began with resolution to pack her bag: it was time for her to leave, it was time for term to start again. She wondered afterwards, when she thought of him, what it was they could have had in common, except the fact, of course, that for both of them Jamaica was cheap in August.

A Shocking Accident

I

Jerome was called into his housemaster's room in the break between the second and the third class on a Thursday morning. He had no fear of trouble, for he was a warden—the name that the proprietor and headmaster of a rather expensive preparatory school had chosen to give to approved, reliable boys in the lower forms (from a warden one became a guardian and finally before leaving, it was hoped for Marlborough or Rugby, a crusader). The housemaster, Mr. Wordsworth, sat behind his desk with an appearance of perplexity and apprehension. Jerome had the odd impression when he entered that he was a cause of fear.

"Sit down, Jerome," Mr. Wordsworth said. "All going well with the trigonometry?"

"Yes, sir."

"I've had a telephone call, Jerome. From your aunt. I'm afraid I have bad news for you."

"Yes, sir?"

"Your father has had an accident."

"Oh."

Mr. Wordworth looked at him with some surprise. "A serious accident."

"Yes, sir?"

Jerome worshipped his father: the verb is exact. As man re-creates God, so Jerome re-created his father—from a restless widowed author into a mysterious adventurer who travelled in far places—Nice, Beirut, Majorca, even the Canaries. The time had arrived about his eighth birthday when Jerome believed that his father either "ran guns" or was a member of the British Secret Service. Now it occurred to him that his father might have been wounded in "a hail of machine-gun bullets."

Mr. Wordsworth played with the ruler on his desk. He seemed at a loss how to continue. He said, "You knew your father was in Naples?"

"Yes, sir."

"Your aunt heard from the hospital today."

"Oh."

Mr. Wordsworth said with desperation, "It was a street accident."

"Yes, sir?" It seemed quite likely to Jerome that they would call it a street accident. The police, of course, had fired first; his father would not take human life except as a last resort.

"I'm afraid your father was very seriously hurt indeed."

"Oh."

"In fact, Jerome, he died yesterday. Quite without pain."

"Did they shoot him through the heart?"

"I beg your pardon. What did you say, Jerome?"

"Did they shoot him through the heart?"

"Nobody shot him, Jerome. A pig fell on him." An inexplicable convulsion took place in the nerves of Mr. Wordsworth's face; it really looked for a moment as though he were going to laugh. He closed his eyes, composed his features, and said rapidly, as though it were necessary to expel the story as rapidly as possible, "Your father was walking along a street in Naples when a pig fell on him. A shocking accident. Apparently in the poorer quarters of Naples they keep pigs on their balconies. This one was on the fifth floor. It had grown too fat. The balcony broke. The pig fell on your father."

Mr. Wordsworth left his desk rapidly and went to the window, turning his back on Jerome. He shook a little with emotion.

Jerome said, "What happened to the pig?"

II

This was not callousness on the part of Jerome as it was interpreted by Mr. Wordsworth to his colleagues (he even discussed with them whether, perhaps, Jerome was not yet fitted to be a warden). Jerome was only attempting to visualize the strange scene and to get the details right. Nor was Jerome a boy who cried; he was a boy who brooded, and it never occurred to him at his preparatory school that the circumstances of his father's death were comic—they were still part of the mystery of life. It was later in his first term at his public school, when he told the story to his best friend, that he began to realize how it affected others. Naturally, after that disclosure he was known, rather unreasonably, as Pig.

Unfortunately his aunt had no sense of humour. There was an enlarged snapshot of his father on the piano: a large sad man in an unsuitable dark suit posed in Capri with an umbrella (to guard him against sunstroke), the Faraglioni rocks forming the background. By the age of sixteen Jerome was well aware that the portrait looked more like the author of *Sunshine and Shade* and *Rambles in the Balearics* than an agent of the Secret Service. All the same, he loved the memory of his father: he still possessed an album filled with picture-postcards (the stamps had been soaked off long ago for his other collection), and it pained him when his aunt embarked with strangers on the story of his father's death.

"A shocking accident," she would begin, and the stranger would compose his or her features into the correct shape for interest and commiseration. Both reactions, of course, were false, but it was terrible for Jerome to see how suddenly, midway in her rambling discourse, the interest would become genuine. "I can't think how such things can be allowed in a civilized country," his aunt would say. "I suppose one has to regard Italy as civilized. One is prepared for all kinds of things abroad, of course, and my brother was a great traveller. He always carried a water-filter with him. It was far less expensive, you know, than buying all those bottles of mineral water. My brother always said that his filter paid for his dinner wine. You can see from that what a careful man he was, but who could possibly have expected when he was walking along the Via Dottore Manuele Panucci on his way to the Hydrographic Museum that a pig would fall on him?" That was the moment when the interest became genuine.

Jerome's father had not been a very distinguished writer, but the time always seems to come, after an author's death, when somebody thinks it worth his while to write a letter to *The Times Literary Supplement* announcing the preparation of a biography and asking to see any letters or documents or receive any anecdotes from friends of the dead man. Most of the biographies, of course, never appear—one wonders whether the whole thing may not be an obscure form of blackmail and whether many a potential writer of a biography or thesis finds the means in this way to finish his education at Kansas or Nottingham. Jerome, however, as a chartered accountant, lived far from the literary world. He did not realize how small the menace really was, nor that the danger period for someone of his father's obscurity had long passed. Sometimes he rehearsed the method of recounting his father's death so as to reduce the comic element to its smallest dimensions—it would be of no use to refuse information, for in that case the biographer would undoubtedly visit his aunt, who was living to a great old age with no sign of flagging.

It seemed to Jerome that there were two possible

methods—the first led gently up to the accident, so well prepared that the death came really as an anticlimax. The chief danger of laughter in such a story was always surprise. When he rehearsed this method Jerome began boringly enough.

"You know Naples and those high tenement buildings? Somebody once told me that the Neapolitan always feels at home in New York just as the man from Turin feels at home in London because the river runs in much the same way in both cities. Where was I? Oh, yes, Naples, of course. You'd be surprised in the poorer quarters what things they keep on the balconies of those skyscraping tenements—not washing, you know, or bedding, but things like livestock, chickens or even pigs. Of course the pigs get no exercise whatever and fatten all the quicker." He could imagine how his hearer's eyes would have glazed by this time. "I've no idea, have you, how heavy a pig can be, but those old buildings are all badly in need of repair. A balcony on the fifth floor gave way under one of those pigs. It struck the third-floor balcony on its way down and sort of ricocheted into the street. My father was on the way to the Hydrographic Museum when the pig hit him. Coming from that height and that angle it broke his neck." This was really a masterly attempt to make an intrinsically interesting subject boring.

The other method Jerome rehearsed had the virtue of brevity.

"My father was killed by a pig."

"Really? In India?"

"No, in Italy."

"How interesting. I never realized there was pig-sticking in Italy. Was your father keen on polo?"

In course of time, neither too early nor too late, rather as though, in his capacity as a chartered accountant, Jerome had studied the statistics and taken the average, he became engaged to be married: to a pleasant fresh-faced girl of twenty-five whose father was a doctor in Pinner. Her name was Sally, her favourite author was still Hugh Walpole, and she had adored babies ever since she had been given a doll at the age of five which moved its eyes and made water. Their relationship was contented rather than exciting, as became the love affair of a chartered accountant; it would never have done if it had interfered with the figures.

One thought worried Jerome, however. Now that within a year he might himself become a father, his love for the dead man increased; he realized what affection had gone into the picture-postcards. He felt a longing to protect his memory, and uncertain whether this quiet love of his would survive if Sally were so insensitive as to laugh when she heard the story of his father's death. Inevitably she would hear it when Jerome brought her to dinner with his aunt. Several times he tried to tell her himself, as she was naturally anxious to know all she could that concerned him.

"You were very small when your father died?"

"Just nine."

"Poor little boy," she said.

"I was at school. They broke the news to me."

"Did you take it very hard?"

"I can't remember."

"You never told me how it happened."

"It was very sudden. A street accident."

"You'll never drive fast, will you, Jemmy?" (She had begun to call him "Jemmy.") It was too late then to try the second method—the one he thought of as the pig-sticking one.

They were going to marry quietly at a registry-office and have their honeymoon at Torquay. He avoided taking her to see his aunt until a week before the wedding, but then the night came, and he could not have told himself whether his apprehension was more for his father's memory or the security of his own love.

The moment came all to soon. "Is that Jemmy's father?" Sally asked, picking up the portrait of the man with the umbrella.

"Yes, dear. How did you guess?"

"He has Jemmy's eyes and brow, hasn't he?"

"Has Jerome lent you his books?"

"No."

"I will give you a set for your wedding. He wrote so tenderly about his travels. My own favourite is *Nooks and Crannies.* He would have had a great future. It made that shocking accident all the worse."

"Yes?"

How Jerome longed to leave the room and not see that loved face crinkle with irresistible amusement.

"I had so many letters from his readers after the pig fell on him." She had never been so abrupt before.

And then the miracle happened. Sally did not laugh. Sally sat with open eyes of horror while his aunt told her the story, and at the end, "How horrible," Sally said. "It makes you think, doesn't it? Happening like that. Out of a clear sky."

Jerome's heart sang with joy. It was as though she had appeased his fear forever. In the taxi going home he kissed her with more passion than he had ever shown, and she returned it. There were babies in her pale blue pupils, babies that rolled their eyes and made water.

"A week today," Jerome said, and she squeezed his hand. "Penny for your thoughts, my darling."

"I was wondering," Sally said, "what happened to the poor pig?"

"They almost certainly had it for dinner," Jerome said happily and kissed the dear child again.

The Invisible Japanese
Gentlemen

There were eight Japanese gentlemen having a fish dinner at Bentley's. They spoke to each other rarely in their incomprehensible tongue, but always with a courteous smile and often with a small bow. All but one of them wore glasses. Sometimes the pretty girl who sat in the window beyond gave them a passing glance, but her own problem seemed too serious for her to pay real attention to anyone in the world except herself and her companion.

She had thin blond hair and her face was pretty and *petite* in a regency way, oval like a miniature, though she had a harsh way of speaking—perhaps the accent of the school, Roedean or Cheltenham Ladies College, which she had not long ago left. She wore a man's signet-ring on her engagement finger, and as I sat down at my table, with the Japanese gentlemen between us, she said, "So you see, we could marry next week."

"Yes?"

Her companion appeared a little distraught. He re-filled their glasses with Chablis and said, "Of course, but Mother . . ." I missed some of the conversation then, because the eldest Japanese gentleman leant across the table, with a smile and a little bow, and uttered a whole paragraph like the mutter from an aviary, while every-one bent towards him and smiled and listened, and I couldn't help attending to him myself.

The girl's fiancé resembled her physically. I could see them as two miniatures hanging side by side on white wood panels. He should have been a young officer in Nelson's navy in the days when a certain weakness and sensitivity were no bar to promotion.

She said, "They are giving me an advance of five hun-dred pounds, and they've sold the paperback rights al-ready." The hard commercial declaration came as a shock to me; it was a shock, too, that she was one of my own profession. She couldn't have been more than twenty. She deserved better of life.

He said, "But my uncle . . ."

"You know you don't get on with him. This way we shall be quite independent."

"*You* will be independent," he said grudgingly.

"The wine trade wouldn't really suit you, would it? I spoke to my publisher about you, and there's a very good chance . . . if you began with some reading . . ."

"But I don't know a thing about books."

"I would help you at the start."

"My mother says that writing is a good crutch. . . ."

"Five hundred pounds and half the paperback rights is a pretty solid crutch," she said.

"This Chablis is good, isn't it?"

"I daresay."

I began to change my opinion of him—he had not the Nelson touch. He was doomed to defeat. She came alongside and raked him fore and aft. "Do you know what Mr. Dwight said?"

"Who's Dwight?"

"Darling, you don't listen, do you? My publisher. He said he hadn't read a first novel in the last ten years which showed such powers of observation."

"That's wonderful," he said sadly, "wonderful."

"Only he wants me to change the title."

"Yes?"

"He doesn't like *The Ever-Rolling Stream*. He wants to call it *The Chelsea Set*."

"What did you say?"

"I agreed. I do think that with a first novel one should try to keep one's publisher happy. Especially when, really, he's going to pay for our marriage, isn't he?"

"I see what you mean." Absent-mindedly he stirred his Chablis with a fork—perhaps before the engagement he had always bought champagne. The Japanese gentlemen had finished their fish, and with very little English but with elaborate courtesy they were ordering from the middle-aged waitress a fresh fruit salad. The girl looked at them, and she looked at me, but I think she saw only the future. I wanted very much to warn her against any future based on a first novel called *The Chelsea Set*. I saw on the side of his mother. It was a humiliating thought, but I was probably about her mother's age.

I wanted to say to her: Are you quite sure your publisher is telling you the truth? Publishers are human. They may sometimes exaggerate the virtues of the young and the pretty. Will *The Chelsea Set* be read in five years? Are you prepared for the years of effort, "the long defeat of doing nothing well"? As the years pass, writing will not become any easier, the daily effort will grow harder to endure, those "powers of observation" will become enfeebled; you will be judged, when you reach your forties, by performance and not by promise.

"My next novel is going to be about St. Tropez."

"I didn't know you'd ever been there."

"I haven't. A fresh eye's terribly important. I thought we might settle down there for six months."

"There wouldn't be much left of the advance by that time."

"The advance is only an advance. I get fifteen percent after five thousand copies and twenty percent after ten. And of course another advance will be due, darling, when the next book's finished. A bigger one if *The Chelsea Set* sells well."

"Suppose it doesn't."

"Mr. Dwight says it will. He ought to know."

"My uncle would start me at twelve hundred."

"But, darling, how could you come then to St. Tropez?"

"Perhaps we'd do better to marry when you came back."

She said harshly, "I mightn't come back if *The Chelsea Set* sells enough."

"Oh."

She looked at me and the party of Japanese gentlemen. She finished her wine. She said, "Is this a quarrel?"

"No."

"I've got a title for the next book—*'The Azure Blue.'*"

"I thought azure *was* blue."

She looked at him with disappointment. "You don't really want to be married to a novelist, do you?"

"You aren't one yet."

"I was born one—Mr. Dwight says. My powers of observation—"

"Yes. You told me that, but, dear, couldn't you observe a bit nearer home? Here in London."

"I've done that in *The Chelsea Set.* I don't want to repeat myself."

The bill had been lying beside them for some time now. He took out his wallet to pay, but she snatched the paper out of his reach. She said, "This is my celebration."

"What of?"

"*The Chelsea Set,* of course. Darling, you're awfully decorative, but sometimes—well, you simply don't connect."

"I'd rather . . . if you don't mind . . ."

"No, darling, this is on me. And Mr. Dwight, of course."

He submitted just as two of the Japanese gentlemen gave tongue simultaneously, then stopped abruptly and bowed to each other, as though they were blocked in a doorway.

I had thought the two young people matching miniatures, but what a contrast in fact there was. The same type of prettiness could contain weakness and strength. Her Regency counterpart, I suppose, would have borne a dozen children without the aid of anaesthetics, while he would have fallen an easy victim to the first dark eyes in Naples. Would there one day be a dozen books on her shelf? They have to be born without an anaesthetic too. I found myself hoping that *The Chelsea Set* would prove to be a disaster and that eventually she would take up photographic modelling while he established himself solidly in the wine trade in St. James's. I didn't like to think of her as the Mrs. Humphry Ward of her generation—not that I would live so long. Old age saves us from the realization of a great many fears. I wondered in which publishing firm Dwight belonged. I could imagine the blurb he would have already written about her "abrasive powers of observation." There would be a photo, if he was wise, on the back of the jacket, for reviewers, as well as publishers, are human, and she didn't look like Mrs. Humphry Ward.

I could hear them talking while they found their coats at the back of the restaurant. He said, "I wonder what all those Japanese are doing here?"

"Japanese?" she said. "What Japanese, darling? Sometimes you are so evasive I think you don't want to marry me at all."

Awful When You Think of It

When the baby looked up at me from its wicker basket and winked—on the opposite seat somewhere between Reading and Slough—I became uneasy. It was as if he had discovered my secret interest.

It is awful how little we change. So often an old acquaintance, whom one has not seen for forty years when he occupied the neighbouring chopped and inky desk, detains one in the street with his unwelcome memory. Even as a baby we carry the future with us. Clothes cannot change us, the clothes are the uniform of our character, and our character changes as little as the shape of our nose and the expression of the eyes.

It has always been my hobby in railway trains to visualize in a baby's face the man he is to become—the bar-lounger, the gadabout, the frequenter of fashionable weddings; you need only supply the cloth cap, the grey topper, the uniform of the sad, smug, or hilarious future. But I have always felt a certain contempt for the babies

I have studied with such superior wisdom (they little know), and it was a shock last week when one of the brood not only detected me in the act of observation but returned that knowing signal, as if he shared my knowledge of what the years would make of him.

He had been momentarily left alone by his young mother on the seat opposite. She had smiled towards me with a tacit understanding that I would look after her baby for a few moments. What danger, after all, could happen to *it?* (Perhaps she was less certain of his sex than I was. She knew the shape under the nappies, of course, but shapes can deceive: parts alter, operations are performed.) She could not see what I had seen—the tilted bowler and the umbrella over the arm. (No arm was yet apparent under the coverlet printed with pink rabbits.)

When she was safely out of the carriage I bent towards the basket and asked him a question. I had never before carried my researches quite so far.

"What's yours?" I said.

He blew a thick white bubble, brown at the edges. There could be no doubt at all that he was saying, "A pint of the best bitter."

"Haven't seen you lately—you know—in the old place," I said.

He gave a quick smile, passing it off, then he winked again. You couldn't doubt that he was saying, "The other half?"

I blew a bubble in my turn—we spoke the same language.

Very slightly he turned his head to one side. He didn't want anybody to hear what he was going to say now.

"You've got a tip?" I asked.

Don't mistake my meaning. It was not racing information I wanted. Of course I could not see his waist under all those pink-rabbit wrappings, but I knew perfectly well that he wore a double-breasted waistcoat and had nothing to do with the tracks. I said very rapidly, because his mother might return at any moment, "My brokers are Druce, Davis, and Burrows."

He looked up at me with bloodshot eyes, and a little line of spittle began to form at the corner of his mouth. I said, "Oh, I know they're not all that good. But at the moment they are recommending Stores."

He gave a high wail of pain—you could have mistaken the cause for wind, but I knew better. In his club they didn't have to serve dill water. I said, "I don't agree, mind you," and he stopped crying and blew a bubble—a little white tough one which lingered on his lip.

I caught his meaning at once. "My round," I said. "Time for a short?"

He nodded.

"Scotch?" I know few people will believe me, but he raised his head an inch or two and gazed unmistakably at my watch.

"A bit early?" I said. "Pink gin?"

I didn't have to wait for his reply. "Make them large ones," I said to the imaginary barman.

He spat at me, so I added, "Throw away the pink."

"Well," I said, "here's to you. Happy future," and we smiled at each other, well content.

"I don't know what you would advise," I said, "but surely Tobaccos are about as low as they will go. When you think Imps were a cool eighty in the early thirties and now you can pick them up for under sixty . . . this cancer scare can't go on. People have got to have their fun."

At the word "fun" he winked again, looking secretively around, and I realized that perhaps I had been on the wrong tack. It was not, after all, the state of the markets he had been so ready to talk about.

"I heard a damn good one yesterday," I said. "A man got into a tube train, and there was a pretty girl with one stocking coming down . . ."

He yawned and closed his eyes.

"Sorry," I said, "I thought it was new. You tell me one."

And do you know that damned baby was quite ready to oblige? But he belonged to the school who find their own jokes funny, and when he tried to speak he could only laugh. He couldn't get his story out for laughter. He laughed and winked and laughed again—what a good story it must have been. I could have dined out for weeks on the strength of it. His limbs twitched in the basket; he even tried to get his hands free from the pink rabbits, and then the laughter died. I could almost hear him saying, "Tell you later, old man."

His mother opened the door of the compartment. She said, "You've been amusing baby. How kind of you. Are you fond of babies?" And she gave me such a look—the love-wrinkles forming round the mouth and eyes—that I was tempted to reply with the warmth and hypocrisy required, but then I met the baby's hard relentless gaze.

"Well as a matter of fact," I said, "I'm not. Not really." I drooled on, losing all my chances before that blue and pebbly stare. "You know how it is . . . never had one of my own . . . I'm fond of fishes, though. . . ."

I suppose in a way I got my reward. The baby blew a whole succession of bubbles. He was satisfied; after all, a chap shouldn't make passes at another chap's mother, especially if he belongs to the same club—for suddenly I knew inevitably to what club he would belong in twenty-five years' time. "On me," he was obviously saying now. "Doubles all round." I could only hope that I would not live so long.

GG

Doctor Crombie

An unfortunate circumstance in my life has just recalled to mind a certain Doctor Crombie and the conversations I used to hold with him when I was young. He was the school doctor until the eccentricity of his ideas became generally known. After he had ceased to attend the school the rest of his practice was soon reduced to a few old people, almost as eccentric as himself—there were, I remember, Colonel Parker, a British Israelite, Miss Warrender who kept twenty-five cats, and a man called Horace Turner who invented a system for turning the National Debt into a National Credit.

Doctor Crombie lived all alone half a mile from the school in a red-brick villa in King's Road. Luckily he possessed a small private income, for in the end his work had come to be entirely paperwork—long articles for the *Lancet* and the *British Medical Journal* which were never published. It was long before the days of television; otherwise a corner might have been found for

him in some magazine programme, and his views would
have reached a larger public than the random gossips of
Bankstead—with who knows what result?—for he spoke
with sincerity, and when I was young he certainly to
me carried a measure of conviction.

Our school, which had begun as a grammar school
during the reign of Henry VIII, had, by the twentieth
century, just edged its way into the *Public Schools Year
Book*. There were many day-boys, of whom I was one,
for Bankstead was only an hour from London by train,
and in the days of the old London Midland and Scottish
Railway there were frequent and rapid services for com-
muters. In a boarding school where the boys are iso-
lated for months at a time like prisoners on Dartmoor,
Doctor Crombie's views would have become known
more slowly. By the time a boy went home for the holi-
days he would have forgotten any curious details, and
the parents, dotted about England in equal isolation,
would have been unable to get together and check up
on any unusual stories. It was different at Bankstead,
where parents lived a community life and attended sing-
songs, but even here Doctor Crombie's views had a long
innings.

The headmaster was a progressively minded man,
and, when the boys emerged, at the age of thirteen, from
the junior school, he arranged, with the consent of the
parents, that Doctor Crombie should address them in
small groups on the problems of personal hygiene and
the dangers which lay ahead. I have only faint memories
of the occasion, of the boys who sniggered, of the boys
who blushed, of the boys who stared at the ground as

though they had dropped something, but I remember vividly the explicit and plain-speaking Doctor Crombie, with his melancholy moustache, which remained blond from nicotine long after his head was grey, and his gold-rimmed spectacles—gold rims, like a pipe, always give me the impression of a rectitude I can never achieve. I understood very little of what he was saying, but I do remember later that I asked my parents what he meant by "playing with oneself." Being an only child I was accustomed to play with myself. For example, in the case of my model railway, I was in turn driver, signalman, and station-master, and I felt no need of an assistant.

My mother said she had forgotten to speak to the cook and left us alone.

"Doctor Crombie," I told my father, "says that it causes cancer."

"Cancer!" my father exclaimed. "Are you sure he didn't say insanity?" (It was a great period for insanity: loss of vitality leading to nervous debility and nervous debility becoming melancholia and eventually melancholia becoming madness. For some reasons these effects were said to come before marriage and not after.)

"He said cancer. An incurable disease, he said."

"Odd!" my father remarked. He reassured me about playing trains, and Doctor Crombie's theory went out of my head for some years. I don't think my father can have mentioned it to anyone else except possibly my mother, and that only as a joke. Cancer was as good a scare during puberty as madness—the standard of dishonesty among parents is a high one. They had themselves long ceased to believe in the threat of madness, but they used it as a convenience, and only after some years did they reach the conclusion that Doctor Crombie was a strictly honest man.

I had just left school by that time and I had not yet gone up to the university; Doctor Crombie's head was quite white by then, though his moustache stayed blond. We had become close friends, for we both liked observing trains, and sometimes on a summer's day we took a picnic-lunch and sat on the green mound of Bankstead Castle, from which we could watch the line and see below it the canal with the bright-painted barges drawn by slow horses in the direction of Birmingham. We drank ginger beer out of stone bottles and ate ham sandwiches while Doctor Crombie studied Bradshaw. When I want an image for innocence I think of those afternoons.

But the peace of the afternoon I am remembering now was disturbed. An immense goods-train of coal-waggons went by us—I counted sixty-three, which approached our record, but when I asked for his confirmation, Doctor Crombie had inexplicably forgotten to count.

"Is something the matter?" I asked.

"The school has asked me to resign," he said, and he took off the gold-rimmed glasses and wiped them.

"Good heavens! Why?"

"The secrets of the consulting-room, my dear boy, are one-sided," he said. "The patient, though not the doctor, is at liberty to tell everything."

A week later I learnt a little of what had happened. The story had spread rapidly from parent to parent, for

this was not something which concerned small boys—
this concerned all of them. Perhaps there was even an
element of fear in the talk—fear that Doctor Crombie
might be right. Incredible thought!

A boy whom I knew, a little younger than myself,
called Fred Wright, who was still in the sixth form, had
visited Doctor Crombie because of certain pains in the
testicles. He had had his first woman in a street off
Leicester Square on a half-day excursion—there were
half-day excursions in those happy days of rival railway
companies—and he had taken his courage in his hands
and visited Doctor Crombie. He was afraid that he had
caught what was then known as a "social disease." Doctor Crombie had reassured him—he was suffering from
acidity, that was all, and he should be careful not to eat
tomatoes, but Doctor Crombie went on, rashly and un-
necessarily, to warn him, as he had warned all of us at
thirteen. . . .

Fred Wright had no reason to feel ashamed. Acidity
can happen to anyone, and he didn't hesitate to tell his
parents of the further advice which Doctor Crombie had
given him. When I returned home that afternoon and
questioned my parents, I found the story had already
reached them as it had reached the school authorities.
Parent after parent had checked with one another, and
afterwards child after child was interrogated. Cancer as
the result of masturbation was one thing—you had to
discourage it somehow—but what right had Doctor
Crombie to say that cancer was the result of prolonged
sexual relations, even in a proper marriage recognized
by Church and State? (It was unfortunate that Fred

Wright's very virile father, unknown to his son, had already fallen a victim to the dread disease.)

I was even a little shaken myself. I had great affection for Doctor Crombie and great confidence in him. (I had never played trains all by myself after thirteen with the same pleasure as before his hygienic talk.) And the worst of it was that now I had fallen in love, hopelessly in love, with a girl in Castle Street with what we called then bobbed hair; she resembled in an innocent and provincial way two famous society sisters whose photographs appeared nearly every week in the *Daily Mail*. (The years seem to be returning on their tracks, and I see now everywhere the same face, the same hair, as I saw then, but, alas, with little or no emotion.)

The next time I went out with Doctor Crombie to watch the trains I tackled him—shyly; there were still words I didn't like to use with my elders. "Did you really tell Fred Wright that—marriage—is a cause of cancer?"

"Not marriage in itself, my boy. Any form of sexual congress."

"Congress?" It was the first time I had heard the word used in that way. I thought of the Congress of Vienna.

"Making love," Doctor Crombie said gruffly. "I thought I explained all that to you at the age of thirteen."

"I just thought you were talking about playing trains alone," I said.

"What do you mean, playing trains?" he asked with bewilderment as a fast passenger train went by, in and out of Bankstead station, leaving a great ball of steam at either end of No. 2 platform. "The three-forty-five from Newcastle," he said. "I make it a minute and a quarter slow."

"Three-quarters of a minute," I said. We had no means of checking our watches. It was before the days of radio.

"I am ahead of the time," Doctor Crombie said, "and I expect to suffer inconvenience. The strange thing is that people here have only just noticed. I have been speaking to you boys on the subject of cancer for years."

"Nobody realized that you meant marriage," I said.

"One begins with first things. You were, none of you, in these symposiums which I held, of an age to marry."

"But maiden ladies," I objected, "they die of cancer too."

"The definition of maiden in common use," Doctor Crombie replied, looking at his watch as a goods-train went by towards Bletchley, "is an unbroken hymen. A lady may have had prolonged sexual relations with herself or another without injuring the maidenhead."

I became curious. A new world was opening to me. "You mean girls play with themselves too?"

"Of course."

"But the young don't often die of cancer, do they?"

"They can lay the foundations with their excesses. It was from that I wished to save you all."

"And the saints," I said. "Did none of them die of cancer?"

"I know very little about saints. I would hazard a guess that the percentage of such deaths in their case

151

was a small one, but I have never taught that sexual congress is the sole cause of cancer: only that it is the most frequent."

"But all married people don't die that way?"

"My boy, you would be surprised how seldom many married people make love. A burst of enthusiasm and then a long retreat. The danger is necessarily less in those cases."

"The more you love the greater the danger?"

"I'm afraid that is a truth which applies to more than the danger of cancer."

I was too much in love myself to be easily convinced, but his answers came, I had to admit, quickly and readily. When I made some remark about statistics he quickly closed that avenue of hope. "If they demand statistics," Doctor Crombie said, "statistics they shall have. They have suspected many causes in the past and based their suspicion on dubious and debatable statistics. White flour, for example. It would not surprise me if one day they did not come to suspect even this little innocent comfort of mine" (he waved his cigarette in the direction of the Grand Junction Canal), "but can they deny that statistically my solution outweighs all others? Almost one hundred per cent of those who die of cancer have practised sex."

It was a statement impossible to deny, and for a little it silenced me. "Aren't you afraid yourself?" I asked him at last.

"You know that I live alone. I am one of the few who have never been greatly tempted in that direction."

"If all of us followed your advice," I said gloomily, "the world would cease to exist."

"You mean the human race. The interpollination of flowers seems to have no ill side effects."

"And men were created only to die out?"

"I am no believer in the God of Genesis, young man. I think that the natural processes of evolution see to it that an animal becomes extinct when it makes a wrong accidental deviation. Man will perhaps follow the dinosaurs." He looked at his watch. "Now, here is something wholly abnormal. The time is close on four-ten and the four o'clock from Bletchley has not even been signalled. Yes, you may check the time, but this delay cannot be accounted for by a difference in watches."

I have quite forgotten why the four o'clock was so delayed, and I had even forgotten Doctor Crombie and our conversation until this afternoon. Doctor Crombie survived his ruined practice for a few years and then died quietly one winter night of pneumonia following flu. I married four times, so little had I heeded Doctor Crombie's advice, and I only remembered his theory today when my specialist broke to me with rather exaggerated prudence and gravity the fact that I am suffering from cancer of the lungs. My sexual desires, now that I am past sixty, are beginning to diminish, and I am quite content to follow the dinosaurs into obscurity. Of course the doctors attribute the disease to my heavy indulgence in cigarettes, but it amuses me all the same to believe with Doctor Crombie that it has been caused by excesses of a more agreeable nature.

The Root of All Evil

This story was told me by my father, who heard it directly from his father, the brother of one of the participants; otherwise I doubt whether I would have credited it. But my father was a man of absolute rectitude, and I have no reason to believe that this virtue did not then run in the family.

The events happened in 189–, as they say in old Russian novels, in the small market town of B——. My father was German-speaking, and when he settled in England he was the first of the family to go further than a few kilometres from the home commune, province, canton, or whatever it was called in those parts. He was a Protestant who believed in his faith, and no one has a greater ability to believe, without doubt or scruple, than a Protestant of that type. He would not even allow my mother to read us fairy stories, and he walked three miles to church rather than go to one with pews. "We've nothing to hide," he said. "If I sleep I sleep, and let the world know the weakness of my flesh. Why," he added, and the thought touched my imagination strongly and perhaps had some influence on my future, "they could play cards in those pews and no one the wiser."

That phrase is linked in my mind with the fashion in which he would begin this story. "Original sin gave man a tilt towards secrecy," he would say. "An open sin is only half a sin, and a secret innocence is only half innocent. When you have secrets, there, sooner or later, you'll have sin. I wouldn't let a Freemason cross my threshold. Where I come from, secret societies were illegal, and the government had reason. Innocent though they might be at the start, like that club of Schmidt's."

It appears that among the old people of the town where my father lived were a couple whom I shall continue to call Schmidt, being a little uncertain of the nature of the laws of libel and how limitations and the like affect the dead. Herr Schmidt was a big man and a heavy drinker, but most of his drinking he preferred to do at his own board to the discomfort of his wife, who never touched a drop of alcohol herself. Not that she wished to interfere with her husband's potations; she had a proper idea of a wife's duty, but she had reached an age (she was over sixty, and he well past seventy) when she had a great yearning to sit quietly with another woman knitting something or other for her grandchildren and talking about their latest maladies. You can't do that at ease with a man continually on the go to the cellar for another litre. There's a man's atmosphere and a woman's atmosphere, and they don't mix except in the proper place, under the sheets. Many a time Frau

Schmidt in her gentle way had tried to persuade him to go out of an evening to the inn. "What, and pay more for every glass?" he would say. Then she tried to persuade him that he had need of men's company and men's conversation. "Not when I'm tasting a good wine," he said.

So last of all she took her trouble to Frau Muller, who suffered in just the same manner as herself. Frau Muller was a stronger type of woman, and she set out to build an organization. She found four other women starved of female company and female interests, and they arranged to forgather once a week with their sewing and take their evening coffee together. Between them they could summon up more than two dozen grandchildren, so you can imagine they were never short of subjects to talk about. When one child had finished with the chicken-pox, at least two would have started the measles. There were all the varying treatments to compare, too, and there was one school of thought which took the motto "Starve a cold" to mean "If you starve a cold you will feed a fever" and another school which took the more traditional view. But their debates were never heated like those they had with their husbands, and they took it in turn to act hostess and make the cakes.

But what was happening all this time to the husbands? You might think they would be content to go on drinking alone, but not a bit of it. Drinking's like reading a "romance" (my father used the term with contempt, he had never turned the pages of a novel in his life); you don't need talk, but you need company, otherwise it begins to feel like work. Frau Muller had thought of that, and she suggested to her husband— very gently, so that he hardly noticed—that, when the women were meeting elsewhere, he should ask the other husbands in with their own drinks (no need to spend extra money at the bar) and they could sit as silent as they wished with their glasses till bedtime. Not, of course, that they would be silent all the time. Now and then no doubt one of them would remark on the wet or the fine day, and another would mention the prospects for the harvest, and a third would say that they'd never had so warm a summer as the summer of 188–. Men's talk, which, in the absence of women, would never become heated.

But there was one snag in this arrangement, and it was the one which caused the disaster. Frau Muller roped in a seventh woman, who had been widowed by something other than drink, by her husband's curiosity. Frau Puckler had a husband whom none of them could abide, and before they could settle down to their friendly evening they had to decide what to do about him. He was a little vinegary man with a squint and a completely bald head who would empty any bar when he came into it. His eyes, coming together like that, had the effect of a gimlet, and he would stay in conversation with one man for ten minutes on end with his eyes fixed on the other's forehead until you expected sawdust to come out. Unfortunately Frau Puckler was highly respected. It was essential to keep from her any idea that her husband was unwelcome, so for some weeks they had to reject Frau Muller's proposal. They were quite happy, they said, sitting alone at home with a glass, when what they really meant was that even loneliness was preferable to the company of Herr Puckler. But they got so miserable all this time that often, when their wives returned home, they would find their husbands tucked up in bed and asleep.

It was then Herr Schmidt broke his customary silence. He called round at Herr Muller's door, one evening—when the wives were away, with a four-litre jug of wine, and he hadn't got through more than two litres when he broke silence. This lonely drinking, he said, must come to an end—he had had more sleep the last few weeks than he had had in six months, and it was sapping his strength. "The grave yawns for us," he said, yawning himself from habit.

"But Puckler?" Herr Muller objected. "He's worse than the grave."

"We shall have to meet in secret," Herr Schmidt said. "Braun has a fine big cellar," and that was how the secret began; and from secrecy, my father would moralize, you can grow every sin in the calendar. I pictured secrecy like the dark mould in the cellar where we cultivated our mushrooms, but the mushrooms were good to eat, so that their secret growth . . . I always found an ambivalence in my father's moral teaching.

It appears that for a time all went well. The men were happy drinking together—in the absence, of course, of Herr Puckler—and so were the women, even Frau Puckler, for she always found her husband in bed at night ready for domesticities. He was far too proud to tell her of his ramblings in search of company between the strokes of the town clock. Every night he would

try a different house and every night he found only
the closed door and the darkened window. Once in
Herr Braun's cellar the husbands heard the knocker
hammering overhead. At the Gasthof, too, he would
look regularly in—and sometimes irregularly, as though
he hoped that he might catch them off their guard.
The street-lamp shone on his bald head, and often some
late drinker going home would be confronted by
those gimlet-eyes which believed nothing you said.
"Have you seen Herr Muller tonight?" or "Herr
Schmidt, is he at home?" he would demand of another
reveller. He sought them here, he sought them there—
he had been content enough aforetime drinking in his
own home and sending his wife down to the cellar for a
refill, but he knew only too well, now he was alone, that
there was no pleasure possible for a solitary drinker. If
Herr Schmidt and Herr Muller were not at home, where
were they? And the other four with whom he had never
been well acquainted, where were they? Frau Puckler
was the very reverse of her husband, she had no curiosity, and Frau Muller and Frau Schmidt had mouths
which clinked shut like the clasp of a well-made handbag.

Inevitably after a certain time Herr Puckler went to
the police. He refused to speak to anyone lower than
the Superintendent. His gimlet-eyes bored like a migraine into the Superintendent's forehead. While the
eyes rested on the one spot, his words wandered am-
biguously. There had been an anarchist outrage at
Schloss— I can't remember the name; there were rumours of an attempt on a Grand Duke. The Superin-

tendent shifted a little this way and a little that way
on his seat, for these were big affairs which did not
concern him, while the squinting eyes bored continu-
ously at the sensitive spot above his nose where his
migraine always began. Then the Superintendent blew
loudly and said, "The times are evil," a phrase which
he had remembered from the service on Sunday.

"You know the law about secret societies," Herr
Puckler said.

"Naturally."

"And yet here, under the nose of the police"—and
the squint-eyes bored deeper—"there exists just such a
society."

"If you would be a little more explicit . . ."

So Herr Puckler gave him the whole row of names,
beginning with Herr Schmidt. "They meet in secret,"
he said. "None of them stays at home."

"They are not the kind of men I would suspect of
plotting."

"All the more dangerous for that."

"Perhaps they are just friends."

"Then why don't they meet in public?"

"I'll put a policeman on the case," the Superintendent
said half-heartedly, so now at night there were two men
looking around to find where the six had their meeting-
place. The policeman was a simple man who began by
asking direct questions, but he had been seen several
times in the company of Puckler, so the six assumed
quickly enough that he was trying to track them down
on Puckler's behalf, and they became more careful than
ever to avoid discovery. They stocked up Herr Braun's

cellar with wine, and they took elaborate precautions not to be seen entering—each one sacrificed a night's drinking in order to lead Herr Puckler and the policeman astray. Nor could they confide in their wives for fear that it might come to the ears of Frau Puckler, so they pretended the scheme had not worked and it was every man for himself again now in drinking. That meant they had to tell a lot of lies if they failed to be the first at home—and so, my father said, that was when sin began to enter in.

One night too, Herr Schmidt, who happened to be the decoy, led Herr Puckler a long walk into the suburbs, and then seeing an open door and a light burning in the window with a comforting red glow and being by that time very dry in the mouth, he mistook the house in his distress for a quiet inn and walked inside. He was warmly welcomed by a stout lady and shown into a parlour, where he expected to be served with wine. Three young ladies sat on a sofa in various stages of undress and greeted Herr Schmidt with giggles and warm words. Herr Schmidt was afraid to leave the house at once, in case Puckler was lurking outside, and while he hesitated the stout lady entered with a bottle of champagne on ice and a number of glasses. So for the sake of the drink (though champagne was not his preference—he would have liked the local wine) he stayed, and thus out of secrecy, my father said, came the second sin. But it didn't end there with lies and fornication.

When the time came to go, if he were not to overstay

his welcome, Herr Schmidt took a look out of the window, and there, in place of Puckler, was the policeman walking up and down the pavement. He must have followed Puckler at a distance, and then taken on his watch while Puckler went rabbiting after the others. What to do? It was growing late; soon the wives would be drinking their last cup and closing the file on the last grandchild. Herr Schmidt appealed to the kind stout lady; he asked her whether she hadn't a back door so that he might avoid the man he knew in the street outside. She had no back door, but she was a woman of great resource, and in no time she had decked Herr Schmidt out in a great cartwheel of a skirt, like the ones that peasant women in those days wore at market, a pair of white stockings, a blouse ample enough, and a floppy hat. The girls hadn't enjoyed themselves so much for a long time, and they amused themselves decking his face with rouge, eyeshadow, and lipstick. When he came out of the door, the policeman was so astonished by the sight that he stood rooted to the spot long enough for Herr Schmidt to billow round the corner, take to his heels down a side street, and arrive safe home in time to scour his face before his wife came in.

If it had stopped there all might have been well, but the policeman had not been deceived, and now he reported to the Superintendent that members of the secret society dressed themselves as women and in that guise frequented the gay houses of the town. "But why dress as women to do that?" the Superintendent asked, and Puckler hinted at orgies which went beyond the natural order of things. "Anarchy," he said, "is out to upset everything, even the proper relationship of man and woman."

"Can't you be more explicit?" the Superintendent asked him for the second time; it was a phrase of which he was pathetically fond, but Puckler left the details shrouded in mystery.

It was then that Puckler's fanaticism took a morbid turn; he suspected every large woman he saw in the street at night of being a man in disguise. Once he actually pulled off the wig of a certain Frau Hackenfurth (no one till that day, not even her husband, knew that she wore a wig), and presently he sallied out into the streets himself dressed as a woman with the belief that one transvestite would recognize another and that sooner or later he would find himself enlisted in the secret orgies. He was a small man, and he played the part better than Herr Schmidt had done—only his gimlet-eyes would have betrayed him to an acquaintance in daylight.

The men had been meeting happily enough now for two weeks in Herr Braun's cellar, the policeman had tired of his search, the Superintendent was in hopes that all had blown over, when a disastrous decision was taken. Frau Schmidt and Frau Muller in the old days had the habit of cooking pasties for their husbands to go with the wine, and the two men began to miss this treat, which they described to their fellow drinkers, their mouths wet with the relish of the memory. Herr Braun suggested that they should bring in a woman to cook for them—it would mean only a small contribution from each, for no one would charge very much for a few hours' work at the end of the evening. Her duty would be to bring in fresh warm pasties every half an hour or so as long as their wine session lasted. He advertised the position openly enough in the local paper, and Puckler, taking a long chance—the advertisement had referred to "a men's club"—applied, dressed up in his wife's best Sunday blacks. He was accepted by Herr Braun, who was the only one who did not know Herr Puckler except by repute, and so Puckler found himself installed at the very heart of the mystery, with a grand opportunity to hear all their talk. The only trouble was that he had little skill at cooking, and often with his ears to the cellar door he allowed the pasties to burn. On the second evening Herr Braun told him that unless the pasties improved he would find another woman.

However Puckler was not worried by that because he had all the information he required for the Superintendent, and it was a real pleasure to make his report in the presence of the policeman, who contributed nothing at all to the inquiry. Puckler had written down the dialogue as he had heard it, leaving out only the long pauses, the gurgle of the wine jugs, and the occasional rude tribute that wind makes to the virtue of young wine. His report read as follows:

Inquiry into the Secret Meetings held in the cellar of Herr Braun's House at 27 —— strasse. The following dialogue was overheard by the investigator.

MULLER: If the rain keeps off another month, the wine harvest will be better than last year.

UNIDENTIFIED VOICE: Ugh.

SCHMIDT: They say the postman nearly broke his ankle last week. Slipped on a step.

BRAUN: I remember sixty-one vintages.

DOBEL: Time for a pasty.

UNIDENTIFIED VOICE: Ugh.

MULLER: Call in that cow.

The investigator was summoned and left a tray of pasties.

BRAUN: Careful. They are hot.

SCHMIDT: This one's burnt to a cinder.

DOBEL: Uneatable.

KASTNER: Better sack her before worse happens.

BRAUN: She's paid till the end of the week. We'll **give** her till then.

MULLER: It was fourteen degrees at midday.

DOBEL: The town-hall clock's fast.

SCHMIDT: Do you remember that dog the mayor had with black spots?

UNIDENTIFIED VOICE: Ugh.

KASTNER: No, why?

SCHMIDT: I can't remember.

MULLER: When I was a boy we had plum-duff **they** never make now.

DOBEL: It was the summer of eighty-seven.

UNIDENTIFIED VOICE: What was?

MULLER: The year Mayor Kalnitz died.

SCHMIDT: Eighty-eight.

MULLER: There was a hard frost.

DOBEL: Not so hard as eighty-six.

BRAUN: That was a shocking year for wine.

So it went on for twelve pages. "What's it all about?" the Superintendent asked.

"If we knew that, we'd know all."

"It sounds harmless."

"Then why do they meet in secret?"

The policeman said "Ugh" like the unidentified voice.

"My feeling is," Puckler said, "a pattern will emerge. Look at all those dates. They need to be checked."

"There was a bomb thrown in eighty-six," the Superintendent said doubtfully. "It killed the Grand Duke's best grey."

"A shocking year for wine," Puckler said. "They missed. No wine. No royal blood."

"The attempt was mistimed," the Superintendent remembered.

"The town-hall clock's fast," Puckler quoted.

"I can't believe it, all the same."

"A code. To break a code we have need of more material."

The Superintendent agreed with some reluctance that the report should continue, but then there was the difficulty of the pasties. "We need a good assistant cook for the pasties," Puckler said, "and then I can listen without interruption. They won't object if I tell them it will cost no more,"

The Superintendent said to the policeman, "Those were good pasties I had in your house."

"I cooked them myself," the policeman said gloomily.

"Then that's no help."

"Why no help?" Puckler demanded. "If I can dress up as a woman, so can he."

"His moustache?"

"A good blade and a good lather will see to that."

"It's an unusual thing to demand of a man."

"In the service of the law."

So it was decided, though the policeman was not at all happy about the affair. Puckler, being a small man, was able to dress in his wife's clothes, but the policeman had no wife. In the end Puckler was forced to agree to buy the clothes himself; he did it late in the evening, when the assistants were in a hurry to leave and were unlikely to recognize his gimlet-eyes as they judged the size of the skirt, blouse, knickers. There had been lies, fornication: I don't know in what further category my father placed the strange shopping expedition, which didn't, as it happened, go entirely unnoticed. Scandal—perhaps that was the third offence which secrecy produced, for a late customer coming into the shop did in fact recognize Puckler, just as he was holding up the bloomers to see if the seat seemed large enough. You can imagine how quickly that story got around, to every woman except Frau Puckler, and she felt at the next sewing party an odd—well, it might have been deference or it might have been compassion. Everyone stopped to listen when she spoke; no one contradicted or argued with her, and she was not allowed to carry a tray or pour a cup. She began to feel so like an invalid that she developed a headache and decided to go home early. She could see them all nodding at each other as though they knew what was the matter better than she did, and Frau Muller volunteered to see her home.

Of course she hurried straight back to tell them

about it. "When we arrived," she said, "Herr Puckler
was not at home. Of course, the poor woman pretended
not to know where he could be. She got in quite a state
about it. She said he was always there to welcome her
when she came in. She had half a mind to go round to
the police station and report him missing, but I dis-
suaded her. I almost began to believe that she didn't
know what he was up to. She muttered about the
strange goings on in town—anarchists and the like—
and would you believe it she said that Herr Puckler told
her a policeman had seen Herr Schmidt dressed up in
women's clothes."

"The little swine," Frau Schmidt said, naturally re-
ferring to Puckler, for Herr Schmidt had the figure of
one of his own wine barrels. "Can you imagine such a
thing?"

"Distracting attention," Frau Muller said, "from his
own vices. For look what happened next. We come to
the bedroom, and Frau Puckler finds her wardrobe
door wide open, and she looks inside, and what does
she find—her black Sunday dress missing. 'There's
truth in the story after all,' she said, 'and I'm going to
look for Herr Schmidt,' but I pointed out to her that
it would have to be a very small man indeed to wear her
dress."

"Did she blush?"

"I really believe she knows nothing about it."

"Poor, poor woman," Frau Dobel said. "And what do
you think he does when he's all dressed up?" and they
began to speculate. So thus it was, my father would

say, that foul talk was added to the other sins of lies, fornication, scandal. Yet there still remained the most serious sin of all.

That night Puckler and the policeman turned up at Herr Braun's door, but little did they know that the story of Puckler had already reached the ears of the drinkers, for Frau Muller had reported the strange events to Herr Muller, and at once he remembered the gimlet-eyes of the cook Anna peering at him out of the shadows. When the men met, Herr Braun reported that the cook was to bring an assistant to help her with the pasties and as she had asked for no extra money he had consented. You can imagine the babble of voices that broke out from these silent men when Herr Muller told his story. What was Puckler's motive? It was a bad one or it would not have been Puckler. One theory was that he was planning with the help of an assistant to poison them with the pasties in revenge for being excluded. "It's not beyond Puckler," Herr Dobel said. They had good reason to be suspicious, so my father, who was a just man, did not include unworthy suspicion among the sins of which the secret society was the cause. They began to prepare a reception for Puckler.

Puckler knocked on the door and the policeman stood just behind him, enormous in his great black skirt with his white stockings crinkling over his boots because Puckler had forgotten to buy him garters. After the second knock the bombardment began from the upper windows. Puckler and the policeman were drenched with unmentionable liquids, they were struck with logs of wood. Their eyes were endangered from falling forks. The policeman was the first to take to his heels, and it was a strange sight to see so huge a woman go beating down the street. The blouse had come out of the waistband and flapped like a sail as its owner tacked to avoid the flying objects—which now included a toilet-roll, a broken teapot, and a portrait of the Grand Duke.

Puckler, who had been hit on the shoulder with a rolling-pin, did not at first run away. He had his moment of courage or bewilderment. But when the frying-pan he had used for pasties struck him, he turned too late to follow the policeman. It was then that he was struck on the head with a chamber-pot and lay in the street with the pot fitting over his head like a visor. They had to break it with a hammer to get it off, and by that time he was dead, whether from the blow on the head or the fall or from fear or from being stifled by the chamber-pot nobody knew, though suffocation was the general opinion. Of course there was an inquiry which went on for many months into the existence of an anarchist plot, and before the end of it the Superintendent had become secretly affianced to Frau Puckler, for which nobody blamed her, for she was a popular woman—except my father, who resented the secrecy of it all. (He suspected that the Superintendent's love for Frau Puckler had extended the inquiry, since he pretended to believe her husband's accusations.)

Technically, of course, it was murder—death arising from an illegal assault—but the courts after about six months absolved the six men. "But there's a greater court," my father would always end his story, "and in that court the sin of murder never goes unrequited. You begin with a secret," and he would look at me as though he knew my pockets were stuffed with them, as indeed they were, including the note I intended to pass the next day at school to the yellow-haired girl in the second row, "and you end with every sin in the calendar." He began to recount then over again for my benefit. "Lies, drunkenness, fornication, scandal-bearing, murder, the subornation of authority."

"Subornation of authority?"

"Yes," he said and fixed me with his glittering eye. I think he had Frau Puckler and the Superintendent in mind. He rose towards his climax. "Men in women's clothes—the terrible sin of Sodom."

"And what's that?" I asked with excited expectation.

"At your age," my father said, "some things must remain secret."

Two Gentle People

They sat on a bench in the Parc Monceau for a long time without speaking to each other. It was a hopeful day of early summer with a spray of white clouds lapping across the sky in front of a small breeze: at any moment the wind might drop and the sky become empty and entirely blue, but it was too late now—the sun would have set first.

In younger people it might have been a day for a chance encounter—secret behind the long barrier of perambulators with only babies and nurses in sight. But they were both of them middle-aged, and neither was inclined to cherish an illusion of possessing a lost youth, though he was better looking than he believed, with his silky old-world moustache like a badge of good behaviour, and she was prettier than the looking-glass ever told her. Modesty and disillusion gave them something in common; though they were separated by five feet of green metal they could have been a married couple who had grown to resemble each other. Pigeons like old grey tennis balls rolled unnoticed around their feet. They each occasionally looked at a watch, though never at one another. For both of them this period of solitude and peace was limited.

The man was tall and thin. He had what are called sensitive features, and the cliché fitted him; his face was comfortably, though handsomely, banal—there would be no ugly surprises when he spoke, for a man may be sensitive without imagination. He had carried with him an umbrella which suggested caution. In her case one noticed first the long and lovely legs as unsensual as those in a society portrait. From her expression she found the summer day sad, yet she was reluctant to obey the command of her watch and go—somewhere— inside.

They would never have spoken to each other if two teen-aged louts had not passed by, one with a blaring radio slung over his shoulder, the other kicking out at the preoccupied pigeons. One of his kicks found a random mark, and on they went in a din of pop, leaving the pigeon lurching on the path.

The man rose, grasping his umbrella like a riding-whip. "Infernal young scoundrels," he exclaimed, and the phrase sounded more Edwardian because of the faint American intonation—Henry James might surely have employed it.

"The poor bird," the woman said. The bird struggled upon the gravel, scattering little stones. One wing hung slack and a leg must have been broken too, for the pigeon swivelled around in circles, unable to rise. The other pigeons moved away, with disinterest, searching the gravel for crumbs.

"If you would look away for just a minute," the man said. He laid his umbrella down again and walked rapidly to the bird where it thrashed around; then he picked it up, and quickly and expertly he wrung its neck—it was a kind of skill anyone of breeding ought to possess. He looked around for a refuse bin in which he tidily deposited the body.

"There was nothing else to do," he remarked apologetically when he returned.

"I could not myself have done it," the woman said, carefully grammatical in a foreign tongue.

"Taking life is *our* privilege," he replied with irony rather than pride.

When he sat down the distance between them had narrowed; they were able to speak freely about the weather and the first real day of summer. The last week had been unseasonably cold, and even today. . . He admired the way in which she spoke English and apologized for his own lack of French, but she reassured him: it was no ingrained talent. She had been "finished" at an English school at Margate.

"That's a seaside resort, isn't it?"

"The sea always seemed very grey," she told him, and for a while they lapsed into separate silences. Then, perhaps thinking of the dead pigeon, she asked him if he had been in the army.

"No, I was nearly forty when the war came," he said. "I served on a government mission, in India. I became very fond of India." He began to describe to her Agra,

Lucknow, the old city of Delhi, his eyes alight with memories. The new Delhi he did not like, built by a Britisher—Lut—Lut—Lut? No matter. It reminded him of Washington.

"Then you do not like Washington?"

"To tell you the truth," he said, "I am not very happy in my own country. You see, I like old things. I found myself more at home—can you believe it?—in India, even with the British. And now in France I find it's the same. My grandfather was British Consul in Nice."

"The Promenade des Anglais was very new then," she said.

"Yes, but it aged. What we Americans build never ages beautifully. The Chrysler Building, Hilton hotels . . ."

"Are you married?" she asked.

He hesitated a moment before replying, "Yes," as though he wished to be quite, quite accurate. He put out his hand and felt for his umbrella—it gave him confidence in this surprising situation of talking so openly to a stranger.

"I ought not to have asked you," she said, still careful with her grammar.

"Why not?" He excused her awkwardly.

"I was interested in what you said." She gave him a gentle smile. "The question came. It was *imprévu.*"

"Are *you* married?" he asked, but only to put her at her ease, for he could see her ring.

"Yes."

By this time they seemed to know a great deal about

each other, and he felt it was churlish not to surrender his identity. He said, "My name is Greaves. Henry C. Greaves."

"Mine is Marie-Claire. Marie-Claire Duval."

"What a lovely afternoon it has been," the man called Greaves said.

"But it gets a little cold when the sun sinks." They escaped from each other again with regret.

"A beautiful umbrella you have," she said, and it was quite true—the gold band was distinguished, and even from a few feet away one could see there was a monogram engraved there—an H certainly, entwined perhaps with a B or a P.

"A present," he said without pleasure.

"I admired so much the way you acted with the pigeon. As for me I am *lâche*."

"That I am quite sure is not true," he said kindly.

"Oh, it is. It is."

"Only in the sense that we are all cowards about something."

"You are not," she said, remembering the pigeon with gratitude.

"Oh yes, I am," he replied, "in one whole area of life." He seemed on the brink of a personal revelation, and she clung to his coat-tail to pull him back; she literally clung to it, for lifting the edge of his jacket she exclaimed, "You have been touching some wet paint." The ruse succeeded; he became solicitous about her dress, but examining the bench they both agreed the source was not there.

"They have been painting on my staircase," he said.

"You have a house here?"

"No, an apartment on the fourth floor."

"With an *ascenseur?*"

"Unfortunately not," he said sadly. "It's a very old house in the *dix-septième.*"

The door of his unknown life had opened a crack, and she wanted to give something of her own life in return, but not too much. A "brink" would give her vertigo. She said, "My apartment is only too depressingly new. In the *huitième.* The door opens electrically without being touched. Like in an airport."

A strong current of revelation carried them along. He learned how she always bought her cheeses in the Place de la Madeleine—it was quite an expedition from her side of the *huitième,* near the Avenue George V, and once she had been rewarded by finding Tante Yvonne, the General's wife, at her elbow choosing a Brie. He, on the other hand, bought his cheeses in the Rue de Tocqueville, only around the corner from his apartment.

"You yourself?"

"Yes, I do the marketing," he said in a voice suddenly abrupt.

She said, "It's a little cold now. I think we should go."

"Do you come to the Parc often?"

"It's the first time."

"What a strange coincidence." he said. "It's the first time for me too. Even though I live close by."

"And I live quite far away."

They looked at one another with a certain awe, aware of the mysteries of providence. He said, "I don't suppose you would be free to have a little dinner with me."

Excitement made her lapse into French. *"Je suis libre, mais vous . . . votre femme? . . ."*

"She is dining elsewhere," he said. "And your husband?"

"He will not be back before eleven."

He suggested the Brasserie Lorraine, which was only a few minutes' walk away, and she was glad that he had not chosen something more chic or more flamboyant. The heavy bourgeois atmosphere of the brasserie gave her confidence, and, though she had small appetite herself, she was glad to watch the comfortable military progress of the sauerkraut trolley down the ranks. The menu, too, was long enough to give them time to readjust to the startling intimacy of dining together. When the order had been given, they both began to speak at once. "I never expected—"

"It's funny the way things happen," he added, laying unintentionally a heavy inscribed monument over that conversation.

"Tell me about your grandfather, the consul."

"I never knew him," he said. It was much more difficult to talk on a restaurant sofa than on a park bench.

"Why did your father go to America?"

"The spirit of adventure, perhaps," he said. "And I suppose it was the spirit of adventure which brought me back to live in Europe. America didn't mean Coca-Cola and Time-Life when my father was young."

"And have you found adventure? How stupid of me to ask. Of course you married here."

"I brought my wife with me," he said. "Poor Patience."

"Poor?"

"She is fond of Coca-Cola."

"You can get it here," she said, this time with intentional stupidity.

"Yes."

The wine-waiter came, and he ordered a Sancerre. "If that will suit you?"

"I know so little about wine," she said.

"I thought all French people . . ."

"We leave it to our husbands," she said, and in his turn he felt an obscure hurt. The sofa was shared by a husband now as well as a wife, and for a while the sole meunière gave them an excuse not to talk. And yet silence was not a genuine escape. In the silence the two ghosts would have become more firmly planted, if the woman had not found the courage to speak.

"Have you any children?" she asked.

"No. Have you?"

"No."

"Are you sorry?"

She said, "I suppose one is always sorry to have missed something."

"I'm glad at least I did not miss the Parc Monceau today."

"Yes, I am glad too."

The silence after that was a comfortable silence: the two ghosts went away and left them alone. Once their fingers touched over the sugar-caster (they had chosen strawberries). Neither of them had any desire for further questions; they seemed to know each other more completely than they knew anyone else. It was like a happy marriage; the stage of discovery was over—they had passed the test of jealousy, and now they were tranquil in their middle age. Time and death remained the only enemies, and coffee was like the warning of old age. After that it was necessary to hold sadness at bay with a brandy, though not successfully. It was as though they had experienced a lifetime which, as with butter-flies, was measured in hours.

He remarked of the passing head waiter, "He looks like an undertaker."

"Yes," she said.

So he paid the bill and they went outside. It was a death-agony they were too gentle to resist for long. He asked, "Can I see you home?"

"I would rather not," she said. "Really not. You live so close."

"We could have another drink on the *terrasse?*" he suggested with half a sad heart.

"It would do nothing more for us," she said. "The evening was perfect. *Tu es vraiment gentil.*" She noticed too late that she had used "*tu*" and she hoped his French was bad enough for him not to have noticed.

They did not exchange addresses or telephone numbers, for neither of them dared to suggest it: the hour had come too late in both their lives. He found her a taxi and she drove away towards the great illuminated Arc, and he walked home by the Rue Jouffroy, slowly. What is cowardice in the young is wisdom in the old, but all the same one can be ashamed of wisdom.

Marie-Claire walked through the self-opening doors
and thought, as she always did, of airports and escapes.
On the sixth floor she let herself into the flat. An abstract painting in cruel tones of scarlet and yellow
faced the door and treated her like a stranger.

She went straight to her room, as softly as possible,
locked the door, and sat down on her single bed.
Through the wall she could hear her husband's voice
and laugh. She wondered who was with him tonight—
Toni or François. François had painted the abstract
picture, and Toni, who danced in ballet, always claimed,
especially before strangers, to have modelled for the
little stone phallus with painted eyes that had a place
of honour in the living-room. She began to undress.
While the voice next door spun its web, images of the
bench in the Parc Monceau returned and of the sauerkraut trolley in the Brasserie Lorraine. If he had heard
her come in, her husband would soon proceed to action:
it excited him to know that she was a witness. The voice
said, "Pierre, Pierre," reproachfully. Pierre was a new
name to her. She spread her fingers on the dressing-
table to take off her rings and she thought of the sugar-
caster for the strawberries, but at the sound of the little
yelps and giggles from next door the sugar-caster turned
into the phallus with painted eyes. She lay down and
screwed beads of wax into her ears, and she shut her
eyes and thought how different things might have been
if fifteen years ago she had sat on a bench in the Parc
Monceau, watching a man with pity killing a pigeon.

"I can smell a woman on you," Patience Greaves said with pleasure, sitting up against two pillows. The top pillow was punctured with brown cigarette burns.

"Oh no, you can't. It's your imagination, dear."

"You said you would be home by ten."

"It's only twenty past now."

"You've been up in the Rue de Douai, haven't you, in one of those bars, looking for a *fille*."

"I sat in the Parc Monceau and then I had dinner at the Brasserie Lorraine. Can I give you your drops?"

"You want me to sleep so that I won't expect anything. That's it, isn't it, you're too old now to do it twice."

He mixed the drops from the carafe of water on the table between the twin beds. Anything he might say would be wrong when Patience was in a mood like this. Poor Patience, he thought, holding out the drops towards the face crowned with tight red curls, how she misses America—she will never believe that the Coca-Cola tastes the same here. Luckily this would not be one of their worst nights, for she drank from the glass without further argument, while he sat beside her and remembered the street outside the brasserie and how, by accident he was sure, he had been called "*tu*."

"What are you thinking?" Patience asked. "Are you still in the Rue de Douai?"

"I was only thinking that things might have been different," he said.

It was the biggest protest he had ever allowed himself to make against the condition of life.